I0677234

Middleburg East

Stacey Fru

Profounder Publishing: A division of

INTELLIGENCE | MANAGEMENT | SERVICES

This gift of knowledge is for:

....

Presented by

....

Profounder Publishing: A division of

Profounder

INTELLIGENCE | MANAGEMENT | SERVICES

Ordering Information
Tel: +27 11 440 7501 or Mobile: +27 82 548 6385
Email: victorine@profounder.co.za
Website: www.profounder.co.za
ISBN: 978-0-620-97884-2; eISBN: 978-0-620-97885-9
Cover design and image, Complete Illustration and Layout by Profounder Publishing and Self-Publishing.
Copy editors and Proof-readers: Victorine, Synclaire, and Dorcas.

Contact Stacey
Tel: +27 11 440 7501 or Mobile: +27 82 548 6385
Email: stacey@staceyfru.co.za / info@staceyfrufoundation.org.za
Facebook: @staceyfru; Twitter: @staceyfru; Instagram: @staceyfru
Website: www.staceyfrufoundation.org.za

DEDICATED

To

Mom and Dad

To

Sydney, Synclaire, Stacey, Shanon, (our dogs; Diamond and Neji), Fru

To

All my readers and supporters

To

Every Child

To

All Supportive Parents

To

You.

Contents

Chapter
I

"Only the desireless can see the world objectively, detached from emotion, outcome and need. But what is the meaning of the truth if there is no love in between?"

Tatjana Ostojic

I'M SITTING IN MY room again, on my bed, surrounded by my books, reflecting on my mother's berating.

I checked the time - 18:09.

This is the second time in 7 days. She always goes on and on about my grades and attitude towards school. It's understandable - I tend to get rebellious because they (my parents) never give me any attention for my artistic capability ... It's just crazy that they refuse to hear me out and that my opinion on the arts is constantly being ignored.

I love my family. Don't get me wrong. But sometimes, their thoughts, or maybe lack of thoughts, including their ignorance of my likes and dislikes drive me mad.

But hey ... can I tell you a stor-

My little brother peeps his head by my door, *"Kato, mom says you HAVE to come down for dinner."*

"Alright." I responded as I walked out.

Our story begins in 2007, a time before your time. Middleburg is my home. A cheerful place where everybody knows everything about everybody. We don't have any major crimes, but there was theft here and there. Everything we could need was around us. As such, locals never really left this place.

When it came to Ms Murry, her life was a mystery. She kept in and lived life in isolation. All we knew about her is that ever since her husband died, she has never left her house. Not to mention, that house, Middleburg East, was the oldest and the biggest in town.

Everybody had to think twice before they uttered this woman's name.

Why?

I don't really know. But between getting chills walking past that house and getting the feeling of someone watching me, the aura around that place was far from normal. I would always hear stories of how brave she was back in the days, and that all men feared her. She fought in the army and never lost a single battle to a trained man, I'm not certain it's true but it made her story more interesting. Apart from the story, nobody knew much about her personal life or what she got up to.

I did not let my curiosity about Ms Murry and the details of Middleburg East distract me from school and responsibilities. I still had friends and I had family that I cared for. I am not a top achiever in academics or the best-behaved learner but I'm really good at art...if only my parents would see that. They are way too busy comparing me to my older sister who always gets good grades and perfect sports scores. Her name is Kita. I have a younger brother as well. His name is Isaac. The tension between my family and I always start getting thicker when the school year begins and ends. They are forever pushing me to do this or that, in order to get this or that.

May 23rd 2007, a Wednesday morning.

Like every other school day, I prepared for an interesting day in school. Our school had no uniform. It had a dress code, which still didn't stop me from dressing like every homeless junkie from the 80s. On my way to school, my dad listened to the radio, while I struggled to concentrate and read manga. I often gave up reading manga. So, on this morning, I recited the proverbs by philosophers who wrote about existentialism. Kita sat in the front seat, listening along with my father and so did Isaac, who sat behind with me.

We arrived at 'Middle East High' and I headed over to class.

I wonder if he'll show up today. I thought to myself as I walked through the hallways and by-passed people who are part of the most depressed generation. Their chatter filled my head and halted my brain function. I focused on breathing because it is one of my biggest fears ... to stop breathing. I ran the rest of the way to class. I sat down, controlled my thoughts and regained my composition.

Thankfully, I saw Wesley at a time of loneliness. I walked up to him and greeted him.

"Hey Wes, what're you up to." I gave him a nudge.

"Eh, just staring at these pages waiting for you to arrive."

"I'm flattered, well, here I am in the flesh! Have you seen Corey yet? I want to tell him about our weekend plans."

"Nope, this is his second day absent...maybe he got kidnapped and shipped to India lol."

"No way, he's probably just really sick. He hasn't answered any of my texts but I'll try him again." I responded, checking my phone.

We talked about the homework but jumped back to Corey. He hasn't been to school for 2 days, so of course, we were a little worried. Even if we joked about it. We had to put our conversation on hold when it was time for our first lesson.

A few minutes into the extremely boring first lesson, we heard a message from the campus intercom;

"Sorry for the interruption. May all students and staff make their way to the hall. May all students and staff make their way to the hall. Thank you."

Our teacher stopped the class immediately. We didn't even have time to pack up. We got into single files and walked to the hall.

Ew! High schoolers stink.

I couldn't pinpoint why we would have to leave class so abruptly; it was probably another safety drill.

Nothing serious.

"Good morning students and staff ... " Said our principal who had no sense of tone, and switched between pitches frequently. This frustrated me.

"The area police paid me a visit this morning. A very strange thing has occurred. I'm sure some have noticed the absence of Corey Maldive and it pains me to announce that his parents have filed a missing persons report. Please do not jump to any..."

On hearing this, I wanted to stand up and leave.

I was disgusted.

I've never thought about how to handle such a situation.

Everybody was flooded with questions, but too afraid to speak.

I sat the rest of the assembly unable to think. The words of the principal had a small party in my head before fading out. It didn't make sense.

As we took our seats in class, I was too busy thinking about what to think about, while trying to take my mind off such a topic.

Is my friend missing?

I may never see Corey again. Fed up, I told my teacher that I had a toilet emergency, and I left the room. I went to the restroom. I walked down the hallway into the cleanest stall. I then sat on the toilet and brought my hands down to my knees. I closed my eyes, thinking about what all this will, or has come to.

I returned to my class and sat through the boring lesson with a singular peculiar thought in my mind. After said lesson had finished, I immediately went up to the person in school that I was closest to, Wesley.

"I was doing some thinking and I know it sounds crazy, but I need you to help me out." I stated.

Wesley looked static for a second as he was trying to figure out where I was getting to with this.

"I think we should help find Corey." I added vaguely.

"Look, Kato... I get it, I'm in shock too but that's a job for the police. We don't even know where to begin!" He looked at me with pity in his eyes.

"Ok I understand what this may sound like, so give me some time to gather up my thoughts and create some kind of plan. But please don't give up... yet." I said, desperately hoping to redeem myself.

You sound stupid for even considering the idea Kato.

Yeah, I know eight but I believe in Wesley. He'll give me a chance.

I had decided to take a look at the official police report when I got home. Maybe then, it would lead me in the right direction about what to do next. But right now, the idea was that Wesley and I will be interviewing regular human goers around the location where Corey was last seen. This so far was the best I had.

"How do you feel about Saturday?" I asked Wesley at lunch.

"Saturday for...?"

"Oh right, I thought I asked you already. The previous plans are cancelled, the NEW plan is to interview people about Corey's whereabouts."

"It could work. But it's a far stretch. Are you sure about your idea Kato? I mean... it may not work out." He questioned.

"No. I am not sure, but we have to try something. I won't force you into doing anything you don't want to, though." I confirmed.

Truth be told, I wouldn't carry on or even attempt to do this without Wesley's help.

"Fine." He sighed, and added, *"I'll do it."*

The days leading up to Saturday weren't nearly as torturous as I thought. I stuck to my regular routine because I hated abrupt and unusual changes. Meanwhile, the only major change was adding extra meditation time to my day. The reason was that my technique of pushing thoughts out of my brain wasn't working when it came to Corey. Or should I say finding Corey? In my mind, I was trapped, thinking about not thinking about it, but not forgetting about it. I spent most afternoons after school in the library reading up and getting more information on the case. Much hadn't been released to the public yet or maybe they had next to nothing, but I worked with the little I had.

Throughout all this, Wesley was slightly nervous. I could see him getting uneasy at the mention of Corey's name. Nothing unusual, though. He always lives cautiously. He is not spontaneous nor did he find it necessary for him to express his opinion without being asked or being put in a situation to do so. He was the most interesting person I know. Which is why I make an effort to get closer to him. I really enjoy his company and almost everything about his personality. It's almost like I'm studying him.

The morning of May 24th, I confronted Wesley after school about our plans for Saturday. We agreed to meet at the park just after school. We spent this school day in low spirits. The students at school had a newfound passion for asking us rather disturbing questions, and for telling us the weirdest things ever, like;

"Do you think that he is dead?"

"I think his parents sold him. Don't you?"

"I saw his face for sale online."

Those were not even half of the things we were told while trying simply to get through our school day. At the end of the day, I was tired of it all; the whispers, the looks, the questions.

I proceed to walk to the library and then home. I do this because I know it'll take me 7 minutes and 43 seconds to reach my home and with my father being unreliable to arrive anywhere on time, I walk. I often enjoy these few minutes of my day. The houses along the streets are fascinating and the silence; despite passing cars, gives me pleasure ... *I wish every moment was like this.*

While walking home, I frequently thought about reincarnation. Every time I reached a certain point in my thoughts, my brain would freak out and relapse, to begin with,

What if I've lived before?
What would it feel like to be dead?
What does it feel like to live?

It was hard to imagine not having thoughts or being unable to feel or think ever again. Nobody seems to understand what I'm thinking and every time I try to explain myself, I sound like my illiterate 8-year-old brother, Isaac. I keep to myself and my other self; my inward self - otherwise known as eight. Eight and I sometimes quarrel, but we make it work and we somehow agree on everything or nothing.

I arrived home at exactly 15:20.

I set my things down as usual and retired to my room. I made sure my stack of books was as I left them.

I lay on my bed and pulled out my journal and wrote about my day.

Then, I changed out of my formal informal clothes and put on sweatpants and an oversized t-shirt. I had my dinner without saying a word - the conversations were rarely interesting enough for me to waste my breath.

My homework always had to be completed after dinner at the dinner table so my mother could make sure it gets done and even if I don't have any homework I would rather sit staring at my workbooks for 30 minutes than listen to another one of her lectures.

When I am excused, I run off to my room and meditate. Following that I rescheduled my Saturday and put everything to paper.

I get in bed at 21:47.

May 25th.

After an emotionally draining school day, I needed and craved mental stimulation. I was looking forward to a brain-challenging conversation with Wesley.

On arrival at the park, I saw him sitting on a bench trying to complete a sudoku puzzle.

"Yoo, Wesley!" I shouted out.

I laughed as I saw him flinch at the sound of his name. I ran up to him and stole space on the bench.

"As calculated, it will only take about two hours six minutes and thirty-eight seconds to finish. We should cover 56 humans on the account of interviewing them and getting their personal

opinions and identifying who may be our main suspect without jumping to any conclusion. You don't have to do much, but read their body language, tone of voice as well as facial expressions. I'll do the note-taking and personal information." I said.

"Mhm." He said blankly.

"Oh come on, tell me what you think."

"Ok well, I think it's all a bit much. Imagine if a pair of high schoolers randomly walked up to you and asked you for your opinion on a missing person case, as well as your name and other details...sounds invasive and weird. If I was in that situation, I know I wouldn't comply." Wesley said slowly.

"Wesley. Of course, you wouldn't. You're way too antisocial to talk to anyone." I said in a playful way.

He agreed by adding his own (rather fake) giggle.

We moved on to a new topic. Our parents were thinking of visiting Corey's family and we had to come with them. We were both very uncomfortable with the idea of meeting his parents under these circumstances. Things like; what do we say? What gifts to bring? What to wear? Had no responses in our minds. Our parents were planning to make this trip on Sunday and we were nowhere near being prepared.

While in the park, we sort of planned out while we continued to talk about other things. This meant more disruption in my schedule. Once I had noticed I was behind in time, I reacted quickly, *"Oh my gosh. I'm so late. I have to go. Bye."*

I didn't wait for his response. I got up and ran home.

Once home, I went into my room and added a quick shower to my routine because of the sweat from the run.

The rest of my evening was spent with my family and my thoughts.

How do I know that I'm real...?

This is the thought that started my Saturday morning. I did my morning routine, then decided to make my way to the meeting point earlier than discussed, so that I could calm my nerves.

What the hell are you doing? Your idea is stupid.

I'm doing the right thing eight.

Right thing? The right thing is to let the police do their job!

So you want me to do nothing?

Yes, stop wasting time. Besides, no one is going to cooperate with you two.

You don't know that for sure, keep quiet for now, ok? I don't need your negativity.

I ended this conversation with eight and started prepping.

Wesley arrived a little before time, looking as confused; but in a cute way, as usual.

We exchanged greetings, went over the drafted questions and gave each other a pep talk - with me doing all the talking.

With 56 humans to interview, we had to get fourteen men, fourteen women, fourteen teenagers and fourteen children.

We started at 13:00 in the hopes that people would be heading off to lunch.

As expected, the streets were slowly beginning to flood with humans. We conducted our first interview with a thirty-two-year-old male. He fitted into the stereotype of a broken working-class human who hates his job but has to put up with the nonsense in order to pay his bills and survive. His responses were also really sad. He was the first disappointment of many.

Completing the number of people, we set out. I checked the time and noticed I was off the set time by 13 minutes and 23 seconds. After a long day of listening and talking, Wesley and I decided to make our way to a coffee shop. We went to treat ourselves and to take a look over the results. As Wesley predicted, we did get shut down by some lowlife adults and teens who thought they were too good to answer three simple questions. However, like any motivated person would go through, we kept on. We finally made it.

On arrival at the coffee shop, I ordered a double-creamed coffee and a Swedish fudge brownie. Wesley ordered Thai tea and lime tart. We sat down and reviewed our results while sipping our warm drinks. Seeing as we weren't looking for suspects but rather information, we focused on the story they told us. Using the notes on their body language, (Wesley's speciality), we could sort of figure out if they were lying. Although each person had a different story to tell, most of them had one thing in common.

Corey was last seen passing by Middleburg East.

Wesley and I knew this had to be true, judging by the reports released and the brief information the school said to us at assembly, *'He was last seen on the streets by Middleburg East.'* To our luck, it was two streets away from where we did our interviews.

The tension was becoming uneasy. As much as I wanted not to jump to a conclusion, it seemed that this was the only thing in my mind. I didn't want to think of the things Corey may be going through. But then again, what could such an old lady have to do with a healthy strong boy?

"What now?" Wesley asked.

"We have to go." I said with little context, in hopes that he would know what I meant.

"Go where?" He questioned instantly, looking at me with a worried and scared expression. He knew what I was talking about.

"To Middleburg East." I clarified.

"There is no way we are going there Kato. Have you lost your mind?" He argued.

"I don't think I had it in the first place to lose it. Look, I'll give you time to think about it. I mean, we still need time to figure out everything, but we have to try. So, take your time and get back to me. Next weekend?" I ordered.

Wesley shifted from his chair. He sat in silence staring at his shoes. He grunted his reply and left the table without a word. Before he left, I shouted, *"I'll see you tomorrow!"*

When he thought I couldn't see him, he started running. Running away from me. I don't know why, but I wanted him to be here, with me ...

I got home and spent the rest of my evening drawing and writing about my feelings. It's the hardest thing to do because I don't truly know what my feelings are, or why I feel this way. I don't know why we all feel so empty in the absence of Corey. I would love to somehow find closure as to why we all feel bad when there isn't any meaning to what has happened. I want to live, not survive.

Somehow, I think that there are two completely different people living in everybody; the brain and the action. Both of them bring out a part of you, with none of them truly being you ... This puzzles me sometimes.

Every time I think, I get lost in my head, lost in my thoughts and every time I'm found, I feel more alone and lost. I stood up, grabbed my phone, plugged in my earphones and enjoyed the tunes. At that moment I lay still in bed and wiped my mind blank.

It took a few minutes before I fell into a slumber. But I did.

I woke up to the smell of burnt toast and black coffee. I forced myself downstairs and ate it with contentment. I later took a shower and wore something casual. I informed my parents that I'd be over at Wesley's home and would meet them at Corey's parents' home. I left the house.

Before hopping on my bike, I decided to take a route that would lead me past Middleburg East.

I stopped right in front of the house and observed its surroundings. Nothing seemed different. This time the fear that would conjure others has left me alone.

The rest of my ride was spent counting the individuals I rode passed who wore shorts. *Six to seventeen (6 - 17)* was the conclusion I landed on when I turned up the driveway of Wesley's home. I left my bike near the garage, went to the front door, hit the ringer and patiently waited for a soul to let me in.

"Hey Kato." Wesley called out.

"Hey Wes. Good morning." I responded.

"Yeah, Yeah, come in." He ordered.

As I entered his home, the instant smell of cigars and alcohol hit me in the face. The house looked too clean - it seemed that everything was put in place and never moved.

I felt awkward at the silence. I glanced up at the pictures hanging off the never-ending hallways. I never knew who all these people were, but that's what we all admire; mystery.

I continued to follow him down until we reached a door that looked like it was made by bare human hands. To me, it seemed that Wesley was in fact very rich. But who cares about money right now?

As we entered his bedroom, I could sort of make out what type of person he was. Everything was dark and jet. He had no posters or decorations. All he had was an ebony bed and a cliché medium study table. The more I looked around, the more it became obvious how opposite we were.

I stood awkwardly as if unsure of what to do. I didn't want to sit down. I was afraid that I'd break something expensive. I didn't come from money, so breaking anything would put a burden on me that I couldn't fund. I made awkward eye contact and shifted from my left to my right leg.

Wesley soon noticed this, *"You can sit anywhere, I really don't care. Make yourself comfortable."*

He should know words don't make people feel good. Still, I sat down on his surprisingly soft bed anyway. He sat down next to me, but couldn't make eye contact with me as we spoke. I get the fact that my presence is scary, but I don't want my friend to be scared. I gently lifted his head, so we could maintain eye contact as I said to him;

"What do you want me to do?"

He shifted back, still studying my face and whispered; *"This isn't about me. This is about Corey."*

Obviously, I thought.

I lay down on my back, took a deep breath and continued, *"Wesley, we need to go in. Think about it... Even if he isn't there, this will provide us with closure. I don't know about you, but I need this. I need closure. I haven't felt the same since we got the news".*

Truth be told, I didn't feel good. Trying to spend my time forgetting about Corey made me think about him more. It just doesn't feel right to not have something that has always been there. Wesley knew that I've been more held up since the news of Corey. I know he feels bad too, but we need to act. Act in a way that will calm both our minds and hearts.

Silence filled the room as Wesley sat and thought. Every time he was nervous, he played a game with his fingers: *ring finger to thumb, index to thumb, pinky to thumb and finally middle finger to thumb, then repeat.* That's right. I've memorised the pattern. I let him complete his thought as I continued to look around the room.

"Kato, I want closure too. But it's illegal not to mention, extremely risky. Is putting my life on thin ice worth it?" He spoke out firmly.

Before I could say a word, he continued, *"I want to do it. But honestly, I'm scared"*.

I was relieved to hear it. It was so positive, filled with *To-Do* energy. Before then I thought the silence had taken him.

"Wes, you aren't alone and I'd like to think that I'm not either. I'm scared too, but I don't think I'm ready to give up on Corey. Not without trying." I responded.

I could not hide my relief at his commitment. This felt like the perfect moment to say, *I love you.* But I didn't think saying it would have a good outcome.

"Let's put this on hold for a week or two and focus on studying the news about his disappearance. We need to gather up the how." I said.

"In the meantime, we have to get ready to visit his parents." I concluded.

We changed into something more formal. Wesley gave me one of his many suits to wear. I fitted it on. He snuck into his parents' room and got one of his dad's many and surely expensive cologne. He brought back this steel blue bottle, the shape of a golf ball. We sprayed it on each other and fixed each other's hair.

Once we were ready, we went back downstairs where his parents were waiting for us. We got into their big black 4 x 4 and made the journey to Corey's home.

In the back seat, we were each practising our words. We were both nervous.

"*It's like he was dead or something.*" Wesley whispers to me.

"*I was just about to say...it feels like we're going to a funeral.*" I whisper back.

When we arrived, my parents' car was already parked outside the home. We all got out of the car and did a last-minute clothing check.

I held Wesley's hand as we walked up the steps, getting into Corey's home. We reached the front door and Wesley's father rang the doorbell. We stood waiting for a minute or two when the door was opened by a woman claiming to be Corey's aunt.

"*Yes*?" She said.

"*Let them in, they're here for Corey.*" A distant voice shouted

"*Oh alright, follow me.*"

We walked into the house and she led us to the living room, where Isaac, Kita and my parents sat. Also sitting there was Corey's mother and his younger brother. Before sitting down, we all went up to his mother and greeted her with a hug. She looked tired. Her eyes were watery - probably caused by the times she cried. Corey's brother, who was still 6 years old, looked frustrated and confused. *It must be hard on him,* I thought.

Our parents conducted most of the dialogue. They spoke about Corey. His case, the police and the school.

Wesley and I just sat around and existed, occasionally we would shoot glances at each other but we only spoke when his mother asked us about who he had been in touch with close to the time of his disappearance.

We had not yet found anything out, except for what she already knew. I wanted to tell her about the small investigation we were doing. Maybe then she could feel a little bit at ease. But like Wesley said; nobody was prepared to start taking teenagers seriously. So, at the thought of this, I kept my mouth shut about the whole thing and thankfully, Wesley did the same.

"Thank you for your hospitality." My mother said, concluding the visit.

"It is a pleasure having you all in my home. Please, keep Corey in your prayers." Corey's mother responded almost immediately.

We all got up and gave her one last hug each, before leaving. Outside the home, Wesley and I waited for our parents to finish talking so that we could go home.

"How do you feel?" I asked him.

"No different. Seeing his mother didn't add anything to the feelings I had for Corey." He responded.

"Agree to disagree?" I asked. Bringing forth my hand.

"Sure." He said as he shook it.

Chapter
II

"If you know the enemy and know yourself, you need not fear the results of a hundred battles."

Sun Tzu

THE NEXT DAY, I saw Wesley at school. I arrived that cold morning to find him sitting down, reading a book. I playfully snuck up behind him and scared him like I did every other day. To my surprise, he smiled and greeted me with a hug - butterflies raced through me. We sat down talking about everything but Corey, or the time we had last night. We talked until it was time for the first lesson. Throughout the day, along with learning, I let my mind ponder.

Hey eight?

Yeah Kato?

I don't know why, but sometimes, I want to stop thinking. The more I do, the more it hurts...

The more what hurts?

My mind.

How does your mind hurt? Think logically. When you stop to think, you die.

Wow, you're so helpful. I thought sarcastically.

Well, I try. eight confirmed matching my sarcasm.

My mind continued with its game all day long.

At the end of the school day, I decided to derail my schedule and use the library. I told Wesley in the hopes that he would accompany me, but he had "*other plans*". This stressed me a little bit, but I didn't think about it too much, seeing as I didn't need his help per se.

When I got to the library, the only people who were there were a group of boys huddling over one computer, and a teacher too busy focusing on his own screen to even notice me coming in.

"*Good day sir.*" I greeted, *ten points for being polite.*

He looked startled and tried to hide his screen - even though I couldn't see it. In split seconds, I saw a brief reflection from his eyeglasses. I could tell why he was desperately trying to hide his screen.

At least now, I can do research without anyone bothering me. I refocused my brain.

I sat down with the notebook which I spent the majority of my night decorating with old newspaper cuttings and scrap paper. This notebook was dedicated to Corey, so everything I found will be jotted down in it. I opened the Search Engine and typed in 'Corey Maldive.' To my surprise, OK, not so much of a surprise, many website links popped up. Now, it was up to me to find the information, select it and write it down.

After a few minutes of gathering information, I stumbled across a webpage in which the user of the site could enter a chat room of their choice regarding different topics and had the freedom of speech. Nothing was censored. I know I shouldn't be on such sites at school, but it was one of the first things to show up when I searched Corey's name.

This chat room was called 'The Missing Boy.' I clicked on it and was taken to the live chat where users were adding their opinions on his case. The more I read their messages, the more my brain hurt. They were saying things that made me question a lot about how this site was accessed so easily. They were talking about his mysterious disappearance. There was talk of a serial killer in town. This mention came up frequently. Too frequently for my liking. One user in particular with the name; 'sickhouse412' said that they had been seeing a pattern. The user posted that Corey is one of many other boys who have gone missing. To be precise, every four years on the same day, a boy would go missing, he wrote. It seemed too fake and I knew this was probably a lie, but by instinct, I clicked on another tab and did more research.

This sick world.

When I pulled up a list of all missing children in Middleburg and surrounding areas, I took down the names of every boy who went missing on the 20th of May of different years.

This was a surprising lot.

This was it.

Although I would've loved to stay and inform myself more, it was nearing five o'clock and I would miss dinner if I was too late. I packed my backpack and sprinted out of the gate. I didn't know why I felt the urge to run, but I ran and I ran fast.

When I got home, I was comforted by the warmth and the smell of my father's good cooking. Exhausted, I dropped my bags and dragged my feet all the way to my room where I fainted on my bed and began to slowly fall asleep.

I dreamt about heads, faces and a crawling human.

I woke up at 2 am in a very uncomfortable sleeping position. My back hurt and I was still in the clothing I wore to school. I got out of bed, changed my clothes and stared out of my window.

I wonder what Wesley is up to... My thoughts spoke.

Probably sleeping and not thinking about you. eight responded.

I smiled to myself and at eight too. I walked to the kitchen to see if there was any leftover food for me. I opened the microwave and to my luck, there was pasta and chicken. I quickly microwaved it and made sure to stop it at one second to the beep. This was intentional. No one must wake up to the sound of the microwave. I then sat down at the dining table and began to eat.

After my third bite, I heard footsteps. I turned my head and didn't expect to see my sister.

"Hey." I said while taking another bite of my pasta.

"Hi," Kita responded as she took a seat next to me. *"Can we talk? I know you've been feeling a little off lately."* She went on.

"Not really." I sounded annoyed.

It was partly true though.

"I have an idea of what's wrong, but I want you to tell me." She ignored my sarcasm.

"How do you know if I'm feeling 'off,' if you barely talk to me." I could not hold myself.

"Kato, I've been noticing changes in your routine. Not gradual, but hardcore changes. You haven't been eating lately and the way you came home earlier was a big clue that something isn't sitting right. We all know this has something to do with Corey. Talk to me." She put her hand on mine.

"Well, you picked the wrong time to try and shrink me. Why are you up so late, go sleep or something." I moved my hand away and took another bite.

"Despite your efforts, the humming sound of the microwave woke me up and I'm not trying to shrink you. So stop being a hardass, I know you."

I was tired and felt no need to defend myself further. Telling her this won't hurt. So, I went on it,

"If it will get you to leave me alone sure, ever since he went missing, I haven't felt ok. My thoughts have hurt me more than ever. I want closure, but I'm scared of what it might come

to. Most importantly, I am scared of getting Wesley in trouble. Of hurting him."

I couldn't look at her face. I instead used my fork to play with my food as I spoke.

Kato stop, you're making yourself look like a fool. eight rebuked me.

Shut up eight, not right now ... I'm too tired.

"I don't know how you feel, but I still see the pain every day. My words won't heal, but if it provides you with advice, then I have reached my goal." She said as she brought my head to her chest.

When my head was well rested on her chest, she whispered in my ear, *"Look for it, there is hope and there will be hope. Despite everything your brain tells you, nobody will know the truth unless it is found. Hang onto the hope. Do it. You may have your doubts about the future, but truth be told, there is no way that we can accurately foretell what will happen."*

I was silent. But then, the tears came. I could feel my muscles getting tense. I never cried. So, why did I feel tears in my eyes?

I tried not to cry. As I spoke back, it was as if I was shouting at her, *"Hope? How do I know how long to hope for? Hope is just a stupid idea imposed by people to make themselves feel better."*

I couldn't sit still as I moved away from her shoulders.

"I don't want to hurt. I want this to end! It's a struggle I have to wake up to every day and deal with. Nobody wants to listen to me when I have something to say! Why?... Why?" I said, as I sat on the floor and curled up into a ball.

She came to the floor, put my head on her lap and said, *"The pain continues. The pain runs in our blood. We are and we create pain."*

"Why can't we destroy what we created?" I inquired.

We lay on the floor in silence holding each other. I thought about it. It was all unfair.

Why Corey? Why us?

The next morning, I woke up in my bed. My eyes were dry from all the crying. It took me a moment, but I slowly remembered the happenings of last night or early morning. I've never shown such vivid emotion to anyone. As the eldest boy in this family, the pressure and expectation from my family never let me be. With that in mind, the thought of how I'm supposed to act around my sister hit. It hit hard. Just thinking back to last night gave me second-hand embarrassment.

I told you not to open up, now she thinks you're weak.

Let her think what she has to, I don't care.

Either way, I still got out of bed, cleaned myself up, took a shower, put on some fresh clothes and went to get breakfast. Although breakfast was a quick bowl of cereal, it was awkward. My sister sat down next to me and acted as if nothing happened. I glanced at her, but still, no emotion. Not from me. Not from her.

When all four of us (my little brother, myself, my sister and father) were ready, we made our way to the car and began our journey. We all attend different schools, so my little brother gets dropped first. Then me. Then my sister.

I sat in silence minding my own business, pretending to read, but really my mind was on the research I did the day before and how it all connects. Still in thought, we arrived at my school. I quickly left the car, said my goodbyes and entered the school gate.

Of course, by instinct, I went to Wesley. With minutes to spare, I quickly broke down the news to him whilst he read the notes in my (our) notebook. His reaction was strange. He shifted and continued to read...

After reading, he said, *"Kato, this is really good information, but the only problem is that we don't know how it all connects. I feel like this is a good lead just not enough information."*

"Me too. When I found it, I thought that it was fantastic. But what now? What next? Or what not?" I spoke out really fast.

He thought for a while, *"Ok, how about you come by my house today? We have a computer that we can use to research.*

We have unlimited, uninterrupted and uncensored Internet connection as well."

I agreed. We walked to class together and started off our day.

It was a few minutes into the lesson. We were in languages when the intercom spoke out: *"Sorry for the interruption, can Kato Sterik please make his way to the office. Thank you. Sorry for the interruption, can Kato Sterik please make his way to the office. Thank you."*

Without a thought, I excused myself. I walked out of the classroom and through the hallways full of shame, with my mind searching for answers.

Am I in trouble? I did not know.

When I entered the room, the lady at the front desk smiled. She gave me a brief greeting, then pointed me towards the visitor's area. On one of the chairs sat Kita. *What is she doing here?* She was quietly reading a book. Suddenly, she noticed me. Her eyes were filled with joy as she raised them towards mine. When I approached her, she stood up and gave me a hug. She then handed me my lunch bag and said, *"Hi Kato, sorry to interrupt your class, but you left your lunch in the car, so I thought I'd stop by and give it to you."* Ending it off with a sly wink.

"Shouldn't you be at school?"

I was surprised that she would do this.

"Don't worry about me, actually. I have to run off. Cya later." And she walked out of the office into the parking lot as she spoke.

I stood in shock for a while, until the lady at the front desk reminded me that I had to get back to class.

With my special lunch in hand, I walked off. After neatly placing the lunch bag into my locker, I returned to class minutes before the bell went off. When I got back into class, my classmates' eyes followed me like flies. Each eager to know why I was called in.

After class, I was ambushed by questions and comments. I answered these swiftly, although I may have twisted the truth. I replied things like; *"Someone wrote me a special letter."*

As I thought they would, they all left with disappointment. All they wanted was some stupid gossip. Maybe gossip about Corey. Or maybe just gossip. I am sure you will agree with me that young teens like gossiping. They just don't gossip.

I was lip-tight after my responses and made sure that I made no unnecessary contact with anyone.

Wesley waited for our classmates to leave. He joined me and we walked outside together. I told him all about what happened last night between my sister and me. As I carried on explaining how unusual it was, I could feel that he had become uncomfortable. Knowing the reason why I quickly changed the subject to our art project.

The reason why Wesley became so uncomfortable at the mention of my sister is due to an unfortunate event years ago. Wesley had (or has) a sister, his sister was only three years old and at that time, Wesley was only seven. As far as I know, his sister had an unfortunate accident and drowned. Ever since then, his parents had been keen on protecting him. Wesley often acts weird when we talk about family or family matters. He acts weirder when we talk about siblings. Nobody can blame him. The world works differently for different people at different times.

We went to our spot and I began to open up my lunch. *This is bizarre,* I said as I opened a lunch bag full of chocolates, wine gums, a bag of chips and my favourite type of chewing gum. I pushed those aside to reveal a Tupperware with a chicken wrap and some stir fry. As I started eating, Wesley and I engaged in conversation.

While talking, I saw a piece of light pink paper at the side of the bag. I picked it up and opened it. As I thought, a letter… She wrote me a letter. How exciting, but strange? The letter was not long and I knew my sister left it vulgar so that I could fill in the gaps with my own perspective.

The letter went as follows:

Dear Kato, my lil dearest brother,

Your life is changing and continues to shift as you go through changing circumstances. It's unfortunate that you are one in millions having to deal with the stress of losing a friend. What makes this worse is that we are all unsure about whether he is gone or can be saved. Your brain is constantly spinning with thousands of thoughts at a time. You wish the thoughts would stop, but they don't. They instead ponder more, more and more. I can't help, but to feel worried about you and the outcome of this situation. I know you have been doing some "underground" research and have put plans in place ... Whatever you do, I want you to put your life and Wesley's life as a first priority. I will support you if you have the right intentions. Now stop reading and eat your lunch! (I spent all night making it).

Don't forget, I love you.

From your dearest big sister.

I had mixed emotions about this, but one thing was for sure; I had no idea my family (or Kita) cared so much.

"What's that?" Wesley asked.

I looked up and hesitantly said, *"Meh, it's nothing just a shop slip that probably got in here by accident."*

"Yeah, ok." He didn't sound convinced.

"You want some sweets? I've got lots to share." I said, offering some.

"I would, but lunch ended four minutes ago. You were too busy looking at your 'shop slip'." He said, mocking me as he was getting up.

He stood above, me waiting for me to pack up. *Gosh, he's right, I'm so dumb.* I murmured internally. I got my stuff and we ran to get our lockers.

At our lockers, I asked him, *"Why didn't you stop me?"*

"It looked important to you, I'm sure it was." He answered as he grabbed the rest of his books and left me to question.

He knew something was up. I got my books and slowly walked to class.

After school, I packed my stuff. The plan was to go home, put my stuff down and only take essentials to Wesley's home. After the walk home, I met my mother in the kitchen. I dropped my stuff and gave her a hug.

"Mom, I'm off to the library. I'll be back just after dinner."

I never hug my mother so this came as a surprise. She smiled, kissed my forehead and wished me off. When I got outside, I hopped onto my bicycle and rode the peaceful roads to Wesley's home.

When I arrived, I rang the doorbell and waited for him to come out. I stared at the door. It was the first time I had noticed the beautiful carvings of life and energy.

Wesley opened the door and told me to come in. He was wearing an aqua blue shirt with no print, plain aqua blue sweat pants and black socks. Meanwhile, I was dressed in an orange and black t-shirt over an old innerwear, black jeans and an ugly pair of vans.

As I stepped into the home, the familiar smell of alcohol and cigars hit me again. I then surveyed the same corridors with the same paintings. Seeing them again made them seem more familiar, *absolutely nothing has changed.* Everything was still in place.

We made our way up the staircase, taking us past a magnificent bedroom which I guess was for his parents. Just past that, we entered a room with one big desk and a huge cushion chair.

"Mmmm, Wesley? What room is this?" I questioned.

"It's nothing but my dad's office. My parents have gone to a gala, so we're alone with my maid." He assured me.

"Oh cool." I affirmed.

Secretly, I was quite excited. Butterflies flew around my stomach. The thought of being alone with Wesley made me happy. I waited for his next move before I could do anything. The thought of fracturing, or rather, let me say, not fracturing anything expensive stayed at the back of my mind.

He then took a seat in the massive chair and started the computer by pressing the power button. It started up with a loud humming noise, then followed by its home screen appearing. He entered a long series of numbers which I suppose was the passcode. Then opened the home screen. He then looked up at me and asked; *"So, what do you want to research first?"*

Still standing next to him, I looked down and answered,

"I want to follow up on those boys ... there has to be something there we can use." I dropped the notebook on the desk.

"The first missing case that seemed suspicious to me was the case of the 14-year-old boy who went missing on the 20th of May 1983. He was last seen taking a bus to the town square. He had told his mother that he received a letter telling him to collect the sum of money that he had won. In those times children were gullible and parents weren't weary, so he ended up going and was never seen ever again. There aren't any leads as to who contacted him or how they did. No traces lead to the boy. This is a stone-cold case."

I sighed and continued as Wesley stirred at our notepad.

"The next boy to go missing was on the 20th of May 1987. He was a 12-year-old boy who would deliver newspapers when he was not attending school. One day, he went out on his job and was never seen again. Yet again, with no leads, the case went cold."

While waiting for his response, I brought out my lunch bag from earlier and took out the treats. I opened the packs and laid them out.

"Wait, I think we have something. Can you read out all the dates the boys went missing?" Wesley ordered.

"Sure. 20th of May 1983, 20th of May 1987, 20th of May 1991, 20th of May 1995, 20th of May 1999, 20th May 2003 and Corey 20th of May 2007." I sounded as if I was rehearsing a poem. But my blood was congealing, as though I am seeing these dates and years for the first time.

"That's it. That day in May has to mean something. The month of May also ... Why May? It has to be part of the motive." Wesley said as he opened up a search engine and began to search.

I decided to write that down in bold; the 20th of May, as a motive.

After researching, writing, debating and filling ourselves with treats, we got more than enough information. But it still wasn't enough to give us four key things:

Who?

How?

Why?

Where?

Most of what we got was information about past cases like; names, ages, dates, physical information and past police reports with witnesses and family statements. No clue to nothing, nowhere.

We sat there (me on the table, him on the chair), looking back at our information to see if we could gather clues. It may sound dumb, but we both thought there was something we weren't seeing. Something tiny, but huge.

Then it came to me.

"If we look carefully, all these boys had some contact with the kidnapper and were between the ages of 12 to 16." I blurted out,

"Thinking about it, did anything about Corey's behaviour seem off when we were all together?" I looked straight into Wesley's eyes, but I was not seeing him. My eyes grew wider in wonder.

"Kato, he did! Corey did. I remember!" Wesley shouted, jumping out of his chair as if he wanted to run away.

His reaction gave me a little fright, except that he immediately started pacing around the room.

"He mentioned going on a date and that he had been in contact with a girl that went to the 'Meek High'. What was strange is that they only communicated through letters/writing, even though most teens use messages. He often went to mail his letters during the weekends. So, maybe he was going to the Post Office around the time he went missing. The Post Office is near where he was last seen, near Middleburg East."

"My sister goes to Meek High. How the hell did we miss that? We don't know if this girl is real. We've never seen her." I added analytically.

"They were meant to meet up this weekend, right? The weekend of the 20th of May?" Wesley continued while still having this epiphany.

"I have no idea. My sister goes to Meek High, and I think she'll help us out! Before I dare ask, ... what exactly are we looking for?" I needed to be calm, collected and have my brain activate. eight cannot appear now.

Wesley stopped in his tracks, *"The letters. The letters. We need the letters. We need to find those letters."*

"Agreed but how? We will have to somehow try and explain this to his mother." I added with disappointment.

Today's discovery was a milestone and it seemed to have gone a little too fast.

"We'll find a way." He spoke back, giving me a slight smile. *Wesley is smiling at me?*

We walked downstairs. He gave me a hug, and off I left. *Next stop...home.*

Be tolerant Wesley.

I observed the silence and enjoyed this time. For an unexplainable reason, I didn't want to go home just yet, so I made a turn. I pedalled so fast; that my calves hurt. But within a few minutes, I was there. I jumped off my bike and ran to the gate of the Middleburg East home. I put my head on the gate, panting and wondering, *how is this the world I live in? How do I live with this?*

I screamed, *"I'll find you!"* into the distance of the gate. Then I saw a light switch on.

In fear, I got up, grabbed my bike and rode off.

At this point, I rode off into darkness.

When I got home, my family was sitting down for dinner. I walked in looking like a mad boy. But I was quick to contain my emotions. I greeted them and took my place at the dining table.

"How was the library Kato?" My mother asked as I was dishing up.

"Yeah, did your research get you some valuable information?" My sister added with a wink.

"It was ok. Got some information and I must say I'm rather tired." I spoke vaguely.

"How are you tired?? I ran 50,000,000,000 laps today at soccer practice." My younger brother replied with a proud grin.

"Ha well, I bet I can beat you and run faster than you." I joked.

I started digging into my feast of rice and cabbage. This menu doesn't sound appealing, but the cabbage was cooked perfectly. It still maintained its sweet juices. It was a luscious meal, but my head hurt. After the short-lived small talk, I took my plate to the sink and made my way to my room. As soon as I sat down, my mother shrieked,

"Kato! These dishes won't clean themselves."

Classic! I thought, as I slowly entered the kitchen. I was all alone in the kitchen ... Well, with Kita. At first, it was distant silence. Each of us performing household duties, but with silence in our presence. The gift of silence was short-lived.

Kita asked a question that I least expected, *"You wanna tell me what you found out today?"*

"It's nothing, I was just at the library reading some books you know, school work and all." I lied to her.

"I know you weren't at the library. You were with Wesley, gathering information." She responded in a smug tone.

"I don't have to tell you anything." Is what I wanted to say.

I didn't ask how she knew, because that was beside the point. Instead, I asked a burning question: *"Can you maybe like help me with something? It's something that has to do with what Wesley and I found out."* I finished rinsing the last plate and stood unsure.

I've never asked her for something this big. We've never been so close in conversation. This is why all this asking and receiving felt too good to be true.

"I mean, ask away, but I may not be able to help you if it stretches far." She then took a seat and indicated that I should too.

I moved towards the table where emotions were spilt last night. I sat.

"There was a girl with whom Corey was in touch with, who attends your school. He talked about her and mentioned her name once or twice. We think that she has a link to him disappearing." I shifted in my seat and continued, *"Now, we don't actually know if she is real, but when we looked back at family and friend statements from the other missing victims, they all reported being in contact with someone that the people around them were unfamiliar with. That is why in our conclusion, we think this girl is that person."*

"Uhh, so you suspect a girl that you have no description of, but goes to my school? Thinking about it makes it sounds like every girl at my school ... She was in contact with Corey but we don't know how an-" Kita could not finish her statement.

"No, we know how. They communicated through writings in the form of letters." I cut her off.

"Jeez, who uses letters nowadays? But besides the point of exchanging letters, you want me to help right? In what way?" Kita complained. Or seemed to.

"Well, if you could try to help us find this girl. Help us in any way possible. It's either that or we dig for those letters." I responded pleadingly, but confuse.

"First of all, we all need to look deeper into this information. Your last texts and conversations with Corey will be vital. I'm not sure if I want to get myself into this, but it's for your sake." She gave me a brief hug and continued, *"You said you're tired. Now, go to bed and no late eating!"*

When I got to my room, I took off my slippers. I picked up my journal for a *journal update.* I've missed a few days, but it's time for an update. I spent the next twenty or so minutes writing. Before I knew it, I dozed off.

I was thankful for a productive day.

Chapter
III

"We ought to be tolerant of one another because we are all weak, inconsistent, liable to fickleness and error. Shall a reed laid low in the mud by the wind say to a fellow reed fallen in the opposite direction: 'Crawl as I crawl, wretch, or I shall petition that you be torn up by the roots and burned?'"

Voltaire.

4TH OF JUNE 2007. Fifteen more days until I was fifteen.

It's been over a week since Corey was kidnapped.

I got out of bed.

This may be the worst birthday of my life. My thoughts expand as I thought about *'The Soul of Man under Socialism'* in which Oscar Wilde details, *"As one reads history...one is absolutely sickened, not by the crimes that the wicked have committed, but by the punishments that the good have inflicted; and a community is infinitely more brutalised by habitual employment of punishment than it is by the occasional occurrence of crime."*

I stood staring at myself in the mirror. My body was bare. It's hard to believe that I'm real. That it's all real. That life is real. I will never understand this ... that's why I love philosophy. Philosophy gives me some form of an explanation of why everything is or isn't. Although opinions are constantly shifting, one thing will stay the same; *the human brain's incapability to understand.*

I made my way to the kitchen.

Oh yes, I did put on clothes. Seeing as I'm early, I find my dad sitting alone at the table reading a newspaper. I didn't think it was a good idea, but I took out a chair and sat next to him. At first, he didn't say anything but a tired greeting. I just sat still and watched his facial expression. There was no change.

"Father?" I asked, trying to get his attention. He did not answer. *"Faaaather,"* I semi-shouted, while lightly tugging his shirt.

"Yes Kato. What is it?" He finally responded.

"Uhh well...it's nothing. Just wanted to - Ehh. It's nothing." I got up and made myself a bowl of cereal and sat down in the exact spot. Now, my thoughts were about my dream of last night.

In this dream, both Isaac and father had an accident that made them blind. I had no idea what accident they had gotten into, but it haunted me. I don't think that I was afraid of them not seeing me, but I was afraid of them not seeing *me*.

The reality is that everyone in this house sees me, but nobody sees *me*. Maybe I feel this way because I long for their love and assurance. Maybe they just assumed that I do not need to be seen. Maybe they think I am happy not being seen. Maybe they all assume that joy came with being grateful for the fact that I have a meal every day. Maybe they think that if I thought of those who didn't have many things, but most especially food, I would be happy. Maybe they are aware that they see me. ... Or should I say don't see me?

"Dad are you happy?" I ask.

"Am I happy?" He answered as if asking me the same question.

"Yes, why wouldn't I be." He stopped for a while thinking. *"If I am able to provide for my family and myself, then, of course, I am happy."* He added.

He put his newspaper down. Got up to make himself breakfast.

"So, is that what happiness is to you? I find it odd because in my eyes, you don't seem happy. You seem stuck in a boring social construct of living the typical 9 to 5 life. Do you not yearn for more? Or maybe even less?" My curious eyes studied his facial expressions.

Of course, I had no understanding of what it meant to be happy, but I did know that my father was still searching. So was I. If we didn't have the need to search for happiness, many of us would not want to live and life would lose its meaning.

"Kato ..." He sighed. *"Life is not always what you dream it to be. There is success as well as failure. There is happiness as well as sadness. We cannot decide our future, but we do have control over our feelings and how those influence our actions. I think valuing our actions is the root of happiness."*

Valuing our actions is the root of happiness huh? I thought as I walked through the crowded hallways. I went to the stop where I found Wesley usually reading. He wasn't there. *Maybe he is absent.*

I tried to find Wesley, but it seems he was absent today. *Goddammit Wesley, at least tell me when you aren't coming to school.* I took out my phone to see if he had sent me a message. There was no message.

Did you really expect anything from him? Your expectations are too high. Keep this behaviour up and you might hurt yourself. eight said.

eight was not wrong, but I refuse to believe him.

I had to find out if he was ok and to tell him some stuff from my sister, regarding the whole Meek High situation. *I'm going to his home after school. We have to take this situation seriously.*

With my decision being the one thing that I was looking forward to, this whole day was one big drag.

At lunchtime, I went to our spot and read *'Monster'* by Walter Dean Myers. It follows 16-year-old Steve Harmon awaiting his trial for murder. I was bothered by the silence as I thought about where both my closest friends are at this moment.

eight?

Yes Kato

Am I lonely?

Right now? YES! In general? NO!

So, why do I feel like I'm alone?

It's because you're too busy thinking about the why and not opening your eyes to the people around you. You're too stuck up in your head - if someone were choking in front of you, you'd most likely think of why they are choking and what meaning it has to the universe, rather than trying to help them.

Maybe eight was right. Maybe I needed to focus more on people and not my thoughts. But my thoughts made me who I was. My thoughts are my most treasured asset.

When I finished the school day, I was extremely exhausted, both physically but mentally. Wesley just had to be absent on the day we have PE. Not only that, but being around boring feminists and misogynists all day sure wasn't mentally stimulating. I could only expect to see Wesley and hopefully exchange a few words.

After school, I texted my father, saying I would be late because I had to pick up something on my walk home. Twisting the truth but not entirely lying had become a habit these few days. I plugged in my earphones to prevent the silence and my thoughts from eating me up alive while I made the journey to Wesley's. The playlist I had consisted of mostly 70s to 90s music. I let the music take over while I walked and danced on beat. I really let myself go. I was having fun and at this moment there was nothing I could do but enjoy the rest of my day.

This is what eight was talking about - living in the moment.

I skipped, threw my arms around, and occasionally sang along. Pedestrians who saw me crossed the street to avoid me and some gave me dirty looks. I may have looked like a crazy person on drugs, but that did not stop me from increasing my energy.

I felt good.

As soon as I saw Wesley's home, the reality of why I came decreased my energy and happiness. There I was, tiredly walking up to the huge door. Just before I rang the bell, I noticed cars crowding the street. *They must have an event going on.* I decided it was best for me to leave and not disturb their event. So, I turned around and began making it down their driveway.

"Excuse me sir." Said a man in formal uniform, referring to me.

I swiftly moved my head in shock and he continued. *"Sorry, I was late to the door. Would you like to come in?"* He was polite.

"I-I, yes sir. I would like to come in." I stuttered as I made my way back up the driveway.

When I entered the home, there were many people dressed in black, all speaking in low tones in different clicks. Classical music filled the background along with the low hums of people. I guess now I fit in with the crowd. Nobody even noticed me passing as I made my way around trying to find Wesley.

After walking past these people and through corridors, I mistakenly found myself outside in a huge garden with neatly cut grass and bush art along with a huge fountain surrounded by angelic sculptures. On the bench next to the fountain sat a small boy around my age wearing an expensive black suit. I couldn't make out if it was Wesley or not, seeing as this boy was looking straight into the fountain it was hard to tell from his back. I approached him.

I tapped him lightly on his back and when he turned, I was relieved to see Wesley. His eyes looked tired and he did not flinch as I touched him. *Something is wrong, he would normally flinch even to the sound of his name.*

"Wesley?" I called rather louder as if he was a distance away.

"Kato, what--how, what's going on?" He said, surprised and looking around as if something was going to come and scare us.

"Calm down Wesley. I came here to check up on you. You weren't at school today remember?" I said as I tried to focus on his facial expression.

Although he sounded surprised, his energy levels did not change, which basically told me he was really tired.

"I'm not sure what's going on and why there are so many people in your house all wearing black." I added.

At the end of this statement, it hit me. *I'm so stupid.* It was his sister's passing anniversary. I sat down right next to him and pulled his head to my chest and continued hugging him as my sister did to me.

"I'm sorry Wesley. You don't have to talk. You don't have to do anything. I'm sorry about my insensitive words earlier." I consoled him.

Right now, it felt like should I say it, it would be justified, regarding the circumstances.

"I love you." I went ahead and said it.

I've never seen Wesley cry before, but it did not take him long to begin. *He's so pretty.* I admired his everything. I wiped his tears and stroked his hair. He was my little baby. Even if it was for a few minutes, he let me see him vulnerable, meaning he trusts me and he isn't afraid of me.

"Kato?" Wesley said after minutes of crying. *"I'm scared. I miss my sister. I miss how it was. I miss seeing my parents happy. I miss Corey. I miss being able to be."*

He slowly got up and looked back down in the fountain. I looked down with him and noticed the fish. The beautiful fish swim along with no worries, no responsibilities. They swim along with the tiny ripples in the water all looking calm.

"Well," I spoke. *"What I've learnt is that we can never go back and it'll haunt us until we find peace. Finding peace isn't*

something that can be done alone. We will find peace together, and if we don't, let's hope we find each other."

At those words, I got up with a surge of energy and said, *"Let's go find your parents. I haven't greeted them and I don't want to be rude. Plus, this will be our first time meeting in a while. You know, impressions always matter."* I grabbed his arm and pulled him up. He gave a little giggle and pulled me along.

Through passing many visitors, I noticed the women had shiny jewellery and the men wore big bright expensive watches. We sure gathered a bunch of looks since we were in such a rush. I wondered what these people were like one after the other. Then I saw them. They stood out from the crowd. They are tall and beautiful. They looked slightly better than the day of the visit to Corey's home. The man's figure is big, about 1.92 m with broad shoulders and a firm face. His stance showed that he was a confident and stern man. He stood his ground when talking and seemed aggressive from a distance. The woman's figure is slender. She had fair skin and a symmetrical face. Her body curved in the 'right' way and her hair was golden and bright. She looked more innocent and had a natural sense of comfort. As we approached them, I became more certain that the man and woman whose back was against us were his parents. This was confirmed when we stopped in front of them and Wesley said, *"Mother, Father, this is my friend Kato. Remember him? He came straight from school to check up on me. He wanted to see and greet you before he goes off.*" He nudged me forward and indicated that I speak.

I walked forward and began, *"Good afternoon Mr and Mrs."*

I greeted them by shaking their hands firmly. His father's grip hurt my fingers, while his mother lightly held my hand and even gave it a slight thumb rub.

"Thank you for welcoming me into your home. I enjoy Wesley's company very much. Sorry if I came unannounced, but I was worried." I finished off and stepped back waiting for their responses.

"Kato, well young man, thank you for coming in and checking in with our boy." His father said. To that, he added, *"We know both of you guys are going through a tough time with what's his name ... Ahh yes Cordrey. With Cordrey missing."*

"Father, it's Corey." Wesley corrected, a little embarrassed.

"Oh, sorry boys, Corey. Regardless, if you are a friend of Wesley's, you are always welcomed into our home." He ended, running his eyes between Wesley and I.

"Kato, would you like anything to eat or drink? If you do, Wesley will take you to one of the kitchen staff who will fix something up for you. I look forward to seeing you again under less troubling circumstances." His mother spoke.

His father and mother then walked off together both linking arms. I missed my chance to thank them for the second time, so instead, I just stood and admired everything about them. Wesley then took me along with him to one of the kitchen staff and asked for two plates of what they were serving. After collecting them, we went outside.

"These...taste...good." I commented in between bites.

We were sitting in his driveway eating Mediterranean Shrimp Kabobs. It was rather fancy and tasted like nothing I've ever had before.

"Yeah, every year the main dish is something new." He sighed and waited for a few seconds before speaking again, *"It's weird that my parents have a remembrance 'party' with people that haven't even met my sister. I wish one day it could just be us together..."*

"Well, I think it's quite cool. The more people who come here means the more people appreciate her existence. Or at least that's my opinion." I responded as I enjoyed my meal.

"I guess you're right," Wesley said light heartedly.

We spent the next few minutes finishing the plate and talking about the letters. After running out of ideas, Wesley said, *"Oh and Kato, don't you have to go home? I have an idea. I'll walk you home."*

I checked the time, *17:54:20.*

I have surely overstayed my welcome. I got up saying, *"Damn you're right, um ... if you really want to, you can walk me home, but it's going to be dark soon, so I think it's safer if you stayed."*

I felt unsure, *please walk with me.* I silently wished he wouldn't care about the dark and just walk with me.

"Well, I mean, I don't really mind. You did the same to get here, so it's the least I could do." He responded.

"Hell yes," I spoke. *"Alright then. Let's get going. I don't want my dad mad or anything."*

He got up, handed me my school bag and we began the walk.

It was tempting. I wanted to hold his hand.

We walked through the streets. Laughed and talked. Often, picked leaves or flowers from other people's gardens for scrutiny. We talked about what type of flower we would be, which house we'd live in and more or less nothing that added future value.

The mood was good so, I went for it.

"Wesley, who do you like? Like sort of romantically." I dropped it.

He slowed his pace and his eyes wandered around for a moment. There was silence.

Realising the mistake I made, I tried to cover it up, *"Actually don't worry about it."*

"No. No, it's ok. I guess I don't really like anyone. The idea of me having to like anyone is overrated." He said casually.

My heart started beating faster, my head was spinning. But I had to grow up. *"Yeah, I agree with you. It's quite overrated. I just don't think I can really focus on who I like at the moment with all the Corey stuff."* I covered up.

"Yeah anyway, I got an idea for a question. Would you rather be born as an insect or fish?" He diverted.

And so, our wacky weird conversations continued until we reached my front door. I didn't know how I felt about his vague response. Maybe he dodged it intentionally and maybe he didn't. Either way, I don't think I would ask a question like that again anytime soon. Not to Wesley. Not to anyone. I actually have no one left now that Corey is gone. So, my chances of asking such a question are exhausted.

"Jeez, thanks Wesley for walking all this way with me. Um, today was great and yeah, I'll see you tomorrow if I don't get killed by my parents." I joked.

We gave each other a hug.

"No problem, I'll text you when I get home. Cya tomorrow." He concluded.

We walked apart.

I opened the door, put my bags down and did my normal home-time routine. This time really fast.

I ran to my room, jumped into the shower, got out, dressed in comfy PJs and ran into the kitchen. I met my family in the middle of a prayer. Ashamed to have disturbed, I slowly walked to my seat with my head down.

I was still quite full from all the food I ate at Wesley's house, but in order not to look too suspicious I ate my normal quantity.

At this rate, I'll end up fat, but at least the food I eat is good.

After dinner, we packed away and started the cleaning.

"Hey sis, so uh how far with the whole letter thing?" I asked my sister.

We were both in the kitchen alone as always.

"Well Kato I'm not exactly a mind-reader or detective, but if you ask me, there is no girl. This girl never existed. Never ask me why, but when you were asleep last night, I read through that notebook thing. With all the information, I recognised a pattern. If every boy had an outside source they were communicating with, then why would she be so young? This either means that these actions were played out by a group of people or an older person. " She concluded.

I just wanted her to finish talking so that I can make this clear,

"Well, firstly, I don't appreciate you going through my stuff. But with that conclusion, I'm slightly grateful that you did. I

haven't actually thought about those. If it is a group of people like a cult, then that should be easier to track down. But if it is an old person, then we're in trouble because there are so many old people around. So, now our only hope is to try and locate where the hell the letters are coming from."

"Yes, that brings me to my next point. If you really bothered to read the newspaper, they are actually giving valuable information. The police will be interviewing people who were close to Corey, specifically his friends and the school community. Of course, they didn't give a direct date, but my guess is that it will be happening soon." My sister said.

"In order to send a letter to someone, don't you need to put your address, as well as the receiver's address?" I asked, sounding stupid.

"No duh, but no experienced killer would be so stupid as to do that. They probably used another address. An address to where they could never be traced. Also, they could have every letter directed to them stored up in a locker at the Post Office and collected every once in a while." She explained.

"So that would be our kidnappers' two main options then?" I was getting more curious.

"Correct." She added.

"Well, that's not good news. Now all we can hope for is that Corey has preserved the letters he received. It would probably

be somewhere in his home or even in his locker at school". I wondered aloud.

"Uh well I think we're too late. The police searched his home sometime last week and found 'valuable' information which I'm guessing meant the letters. Of course, I can't be sure, but what else could it be?" My sister seemed to be well informed.

"Wha- Why didn't you tell us sooner!" I shouted in distress while tugging at my hair.

This is a big deal. If those letters aren't there, then our chances become way slimmer than before.

"Kato. Listen! I didn't tell you because you still have a chance of finding it out." She pleaded.

"How?" I asked in a calm tone.

"Well obviously through the police interview. I'm certain that they will present you with the letters. They may be indirect, but you have a chance. Also, when you go in, be extra careful because fake copies of the letter may be used." She was sounding like a detective now.

"If that's the case, I've got to be fully prepared. I know I'm innocent, but it's totally normal for a person to feel even a little scared or guilty sometimes. This interrogation could happen anytime soon." I pondered loudly.

"It could, and it should. The police shouldn't hold up any type of leads in a missing persons case." Kita replied.

I reacted immediately, stating, *"So far, we can't judge their actions. It must be hard on them since they have next to nothing to work with. I wonder what it's like to work in the police force ..."*

"Same." She spoke.

"Well then we can both wonder all the way into bed." My joke did not sound as funny as it did to me.

"Fine-uh." She concluded.

With those words, I hugged Kita good night and briskly walked off to my room.

I realised after the conversation that it was the most informative talk that I've had about Corey so far. *I miss you, Corey.*

I remembered that Wesley promised me a text to say he got home safely. I checked my phone, but nothing had reached my inbox, YET. I was worried, but with the little I could do, I thought it best to wait. And so, I did. I sat on my bed just waiting for his text. I decided I will not sleep until he atones to his promise. Although it might sound cocky, I was in fact worried about him. I really tried not to, but the thoughts of losing him like I did Corey slowly crushed my brain. *Wesley won't leave me, he can't.*

I grabbed my sketchbook and started furiously drawing. The more I thought about Wesley getting lost as well, the harder and faster I drew. I thought the thoughts would kill me. But I soon realised how stupid and foolish I am. I threw everything including my phone on the floor and curled up in bed.

My bed was warm and gave me an odd sense of feeling welcomed.

When I woke up, I had no motivation. Nothing to drive me to go to school. I wanted to stay where I was, but Wesley. Would Wesley do this for me? I was questioning. For me, it's the issue of commitment. I try too hard or maybe I don't try hard enough. Maybe I look for some type of meaningful and challenging relationship when I don't know how to communicate the dedication I have. Or maybe, just maybe I'm incapable of keeping a steady friendship.

Whatever the conclusion is, I can only know at the end. Not the end of my life or the end of the day, but at the end of each friendship. I evaluate the roles and how each person contributed to the bigger picture that made our interactions so unique. What made them different from everyone and everything else?

For example, Corey. We were both very close to each other. We shared special moments and had exciting memories. He was more outgoing and very sociable. He didn't take things to heart and valued doing eventful things to having conversations. I guess that's what made him an easy target for the kidnapper, murderer, or thief. I guess he got bored with routines and was out chasing his next high ... in the form of a girl. Whatever I contributed to the relationship was more sophisticated. I am less of a risk-taker and enjoy thinking things through. I was there more emotionally than physically. I made the conclusion that I cared more for him than he did for me, but he valued the emotional support so much that (if the roles were switched), would drive him to show commitment.

I decided I would go to school, after the conversation I had with my sister last night. There was much to be shared with Wesley. That will only happen if he made it home alive or if he would make the choice to show up to school.

I performed my morning routine slowly. I was in no rush. The rest of my family members were running around doing this or that. I would be too if I had something to keep me going. I had unfortunately managed to skip breakfast which was also my favourite meal of the day. This day was off to a bad start. I got into the car, took out a novel and turned off any will to socialise. When we arrived at school like I do every school day, I got out of the car and said goodbye, then entered a building full of young minds and old minds who are fighting to condition these young minds. To my relief there Wesley was, sitting in the exact spot, doing the exact same thing he does every morning. I walked up behind him and gave him a scare. It works every single time. I thought that by now, he would be immune to my childish ways. But he still jumps up a little and gives a small startled shout each time. Although he doesn't turn around to verify if I am the one, he still calms down and returns to his usual ways. I sat down next to him and observed him for a second or two before hesitantly confronting him; *"I thought you were dead."*

"Kato, what the hell? Don't play around with that word." He gently fought back.

Oh right ... his sister's memorial. *"Oh damn, I'm sorry. It's just, I didn't get the promised text saying you were ok".* I startled.

"Well then, why don't you ask now?" He put down what he was reading and stared straight in the eyes.

He was obviously offended and for the first time, he showed some type of conversational contact. However, he showed it for all the wrong reasons.

I didn't know what to do next, and I had no time to think. But I decided on asking, *"Well, Wesley. Are you ok?"*

"Don't give me that Kato. You know damn well I have no reason to be. In times where everything is going wrong, you seem to be too calm. I don't have the support system you have. I really expected you to understand." He attempted to walk away, but there was no reason for the bell had begun to ring.

See, this might be one of the worst days ever.

For a naive teenager, I thought a lot. I was aware I had a big internal ego. I made great assumptions about what every situation I was in should be like; like now with Wesley. I expected him to brush this off and give a playful apology. I didn't consider his side and what he would be feeling. Is this fair? I am not sure. But I can assure you that this made me seem like a bad person. A person who doesn't care. Although I have no excuse, it's like I failed the test to operate 'normally' and of course, 'normal' people wouldn't understand. We all have different brains that work differently. I don't expect yours to understand what mine puts me through, but I expect you to be considerate. Yet myself, I do not consider what yours might be going through.

When break soon approached, I wanted to talk to Wesley. I wanted to apologise. He spoiled all those plans when he didn't show up to our regular spot. Which was like a huge kick in the stomach. This action indicated that he wanted nothing to do with me. I sat down in the spot alone and ate my lunch. I got bored easily and fumbled around my bag for my sketchbook. When I didn't find it, I quickly recalled the events of last night. I figured it was laying down in the same spot I threw it in in my bedroom. So, I was forced to read. It wasn't something ideal for me to do. So, I didn't. I sat down staring at the ground. No appetite, nothing. These are the moments when I just feel like screaming ... no, even more like hurting someone. But I can't, without going to jail or without legal punishment. So, the only person I can hurt without suffering consequences is myself. There are many forms of self-harm. Just because this one isn't visible doesn't mean it doesn't exist.

I hate today!

I hated it from the start, but the fact that Wesley won't even look at me in class makes me want to cry. We sit next to each other in nearly every lesson. This is the first time I've seen him visibly ignore my gestures to get him to talk. He is being a total brat about this. Apart from knowing that he is my only friend and confidant, he also knows that we only have each other when it comes to finding closure about Corey. The more time we waste, the more harm could be inflicted on our dear friend. At this moment, he didn't seem to care. My last attempt at talking to him would be after school. If that doesn't work, then I guess we will have to put everything on finding Corey on hold. *Wesley is extremely self-fish.* I could be a little bit harsh in judging him, but yes, it was true.

After a whole day filled with boredom at school, anger and confusion had come to an end and the last chance of getting through him was now. I waited patiently for him to finish as he packed his stuff away. I then ambushed him as he was stepping out.

"Wesley, stop and listen to me!" I said.

He didn't react, so I grabbed his arm and pulled him up to me,

"I need you to stop. Never mind. Not only me. We all need you to stop. I get it, you're angry, but is it really worth the while? This whole thing is about cooperation. I'm sorry I spoke to you the way I did, but I would have never hoped of this outcome. I just want peace so we can move on ... please?"

He seemed calm but stayed silent, *"Wesley please talk to me."*

"God! Kato, not everything is about 'we'. Don't use 'we' so much that I lose who I am because I'm chasing your godforsaken dream. I understand you're sorry, but this is a problem I have to deal with. You can't help because this has nothing to do with you. We've both put our lives on hold trying to help or to find Corey. He needs our help, but what about us? We need to be seen at some point. I can't keep on. I'm tired Kato." He burst out.

"Wesley ... " I said as I gave him a tight hug, *"We can do this. I know it's crazy. We're both new to the narrative, but Corey... It's For Corey."* I pleaded.

"Do you think Corey would do the same if it was one of us? Uh Kato?" He questioned, while we were still hugging.

"Wel-" I attempted to speak, but he cut in.

"No, he wouldn't. He would make excuses upon excuses. He would probably let the police do their job while he lives on normally. You have to realise and identify when you come into a one-sided relationship. You're being way too naïve." He spoke as he pulled apart.

"That's being self-fish. You can't not do something because the same wouldn't be done for you. Ever thought that's why he is the one missing? Because he wouldn't do the same for another?" I reacted.

"Ok look. I care about this. I really do. But can you give me a break? I need some time to be taken away, so I can survive this whole thing mentally. Maybe not even tomorrow ... the day after?" Wesley requested.

"Yeah, sure whatever." I studied his face one and left.

I didn't look back because to me, this new Wesley didn't exist. Maybe until his little 'break' is entirely over? All the information I had wanted to tell him had gone to waste, because of his act. I must give it to him. He's a good actor. Or maybe he is not an actor. Maybe what I saw today was the real Wesley. The new version ... this real version of him is possibly one of the last people I want to be around. For some odd reason, I was looking forward to tonight's conversation with Kita. My feelings towards her have changed dramatically since she confronted me. I used to think of her as someone who was silly and weird, but now,

I see her as someone I can talk to and share good interactions with. At least one of my relationships was going up.

I stopped sprinting after a while because although I had made it far away from the school, I am not a fit person. I was still extremely tired. I walked the rest of the way home with my hands on my head whilst breathing heavily. The outfit I wore today was not for whatever I thought I was doing. When I got home, I performed my usual routine and stopped for a snack before doing homework.

I got the smell of something getting cooked up in the kitchen. At that, I changed into my PJs and waited for the call. While waiting for mealtime, I noticed my sketchbook from last night on the floor, laying open but facing down. I picked it up to tidy it away, but when I turned it over, I was ... shocked. I didn't recall what on earth I was drawing until this very moment. On the page were two faces in a rough sketch. One face was mine the other was Wesley. Wesley's face was crying while mine just looked at him failing to get through to him. It felt too real. I didn't like it. I swiftly closed the book and refused to think about what I saw anymore.

"Kato, eating time!" My mother shouted out.

Her call sounded too loud. But there was my call.

I left.

I got to the table and enjoyed my meal in silence. Everything after that was sort of rushed, so I could get everybody out of the kitchen and be left with my sister.

Once we were alone and had finished evening chores, we both sat down by instinct.

She initiated the conversation, *"So, tell me about your day. I noticed this morning you were off to a rather slow start. You even missed breakfast, isn't that your favourite meal of the day."*

She really does pay attention, I thought before responding, *"Funny you ask because today was possibly one of the worst days I've had."*

"Well then, don't keep it to yourself, tell moi." She sounded stern.

I reacted to that. I proceeded to tell her everything, starting from the memorial yesterday, leading up to school today. I didn't realise how bad I was at storytelling. As I continued, I saw no emotion or reaction from my sister. She sat still, looking at me. Somehow, I knew she was listening. I concluded and awaited her response.

"Well, it sounds like petty boy drama. No. I am not dismissing your emotions, but I'm just saying it will surely pass. Not in taking sides, but maybe give Wesley some space. I mean with the stuff regarding his sister, maybe he needs all the space he can get. You both must be overwhelmed. I suggest

you take a break with him. Once you guys have found your feet again, we will go into this thing in full blast." She advised.

She made some sense, but how can I hold on? I tried to keep quiet, but no, I can't. Corey may be in big trouble. That is if he is still alive.

This thought gave me strength to add, *"But we're running out of time. It's been eight days since he was last seen and I'm worried. We have to plan the break-in soon."* I forgot she had no idea about the break-in plan.

"Kato, what break-in plan?" She sounded really shocked.

"U-u-uh well, you see, it's just an idea. Nothing too serious. Wes and I are going to investigate somewhere. Nothing dangerous, lol." I tried to speak lightly.

"Investigate where?" Her voice hardened (sound can't really harden, but hers did). She sounded like she wasn't playing any games.

"Middleburg East." I said with my head down, trying to avoid eye contact.

"Are you crazy? Kato! Are you crazy!" She rebuked in a hushed voice.

Of course, she was making sure she didn't cause a scene that will invite our parents to emerge.

"Listen, she's been doing it. There aren't any signs of a group of people and like you said, who on earth uses letters? Of course,

unless they are really old." I was stating facts, but she refused to acknowledge my voice.

Rather, she added, *"You could get hurt or go to jail. I never said she wasn't a suspect, but the thought of you and your friend entering that hell-bound house is crazy."*

"C'mon Kita. It's the only way we will know for sure. I swear, all we need is a plan and of course, you backing us up." I paused and carried on; *"We found blueprints of the home when it was getting built with details of all the rooms, hallways and others."*

"How?" She asked in disbelief.

"I mean the library had a book with all the town's old infrastructure, so we, I mean I just tore out the page on Middleburg East." I clarified.

"I don't know what to say. I'll think this over. How about after we've all taken a break away from this thing, we can meet up on Friday here and talk about what on earth is going to happen and how we will move forward." She said.

"Sounds like a good deal." I ended.

But before leaving, curiosity got me. So, I asked, *"Why are you helping out so much?"*

"Easy, I don't want to live with the guilt of something happening to you." She was snappy.

"Too specific. Well, good night."

"Yeah, sleep tight." She spewed back.

Another meaningful conversation with my sister. Now I'm seriously considering dropping Wesley and taking up Kita as my new partner on this case. But I don't think I'm that cruel. Although I wouldn't mind. Lately, Wesley hasn't been it. If he was going to let his emotions get in the way of me saving my friend, then he has to go.

With those last thoughts, I drifted off into the sleep universe.

Chapter
IV

"Life can only be understood backwards; but it must be lived forwards".

Soren Kierkegaard

I woke up around 3:00 am.

I just couldn't rest easily. I didn't know by what means or how I was going to survive another day in school without someone to interact with.

I thought about how Wesley would. He seemed to do just fine yesterday, so I erased the thought. *Today is about me. Not about him. Just school and myself.*

I couldn't sleep. My eyes were burning just by staying open. I lay in my bed in the dark, flinching at every sound I heard. I soon formed a fantasy about my family being robbed at gunpoint. In my thoughts, all of us were with our hands tied behind our backs and mouths gagged. I let this thought progress to the point where I couldn't sleep. I was hearing gunshots and footsteps. As the shooting and steps progressed, I realised that I couldn't take it any longer. I got out of bed and went to the kitchen. The noises followed me. I sat on the kitchen stool, waiting for the noises to ease. I was scared. I didn't want to bother anyone, so I pretended that I was a security guard waiting for criminals to approach the land ... my land. In each of my hands were a meat knife and a frying pan. *No one will be able to threaten my family without me interfering.*

Am I a little bit childish?

Maybe, but it was entertaining.

This was not a dream as I was not sleeping. I was not daydreaming as well. I was just thinking. These were thoughts that felt like a dream.

After what seemed like hours, I made my way back to my bedroom. I had to try and sleep again. My brain hurt. My eyes hurt. I couldn't take it. Even if sleep wouldn't take me, I'll lay in my bed until it does.

In the end, after hours of trying to sleep, sleep agreed to take me. But I, unfortunately, have school.

I woke up nearly an hour later than usual.

When I attempted to roll over, I hit my head on the same pan sworn to protect me. I took that as a waking call and got out of bed. I did my usual, but today was another day of no breakfast.

I don't feel like myself.

Maybe it was my lack of sleep, but today was not my day ... Again. I don't think that I'll make it through this whole week without breaking down. Everything is moving so fast and I can't catch up. When I left the front door, and felt the breeze. I knew I was in for a bad time. I got into the car.

As the car moved, I made an effort to read. Unfortunately, I quickly drifted into sleep while reading. Within those short minutes, I dreamt and hoped about not going to school. About not having a day full of fun and wonder. I think I got ahead of myself because as soon as I saw the school, I knew that today was not the day I followed any rules.

"Father, do you think I could get some money?" I asked my dad for a large, but not suspicious sum of money.

"Here here, have a good day." He responded handing me notes

"Thank you, you too!" I said my thanks and pretended to walk into the building. Instead, I stood outside for a while and waited for the car to drive off. I casually pocketed the money, looked around and walked back towards my home. I had no plan whatsoever in mind, but as long as I avoid three things; school, Kita and Wesley, I should be able to have a carefree day.

It was rather early in the morning, so the surrounding areas around the school were still quiet. This made it easier for me to ease off suspicion. I knew I didn't look like an adult who was wandering the streets on a Wednesday morning, but I didn't look like a fourteen-year-old either. I just created a scenario in my head. If asked why I'm not in school, I'd simply say that they have no right to ask me anything. Would it work?

Maybe not. But I was unusually optimistic. I had seven free hours on my hands and within the first few minutes, I was already tired. I figured I'd sneak back home and take a quick nap before really enjoying my day.

My mother had a part-time job as a massage therapist along with being a stay-at-home mother. Since Monday, she has been booked with gigs at a school in another town. So, she would not be home for the next few hours. So far, my luck was booming. Everyone would be out of the home. Which sounded great to me.

Up until I remembered my dark fantasy about being robbed, I was fine with the thought of being alone. As my thoughts paid out, it dawned on me. This time I would be alone, with no power in numbers. The more steps I took towards my home, the more I didn't want to move.

But I was tired and it was highly unlikely that a robbery would happen.

I weighed my options and decided that I would step up and just take a quick little nap. I was tired after all and didn't get the sleep I desired, so to me, this felt very well deserved. Call me crazy but I take risks (sometimes).

When I got home, I couldn't enter through the front door because the door was locked; obviously, because nobody was home. My family didn't keep an extra key hidden somewhere. As you know, that only happens in the movies.

I was stranded outside my house thinking. If anyone was to pass and see me just staring the house, they'd probably think that I was trying to steal or something. So, I decided to find an open window. I was using my size to my advantage. I was rather slender, so trying to fit in one of the back windows was my best bet.

Soon enough, I found an opened window which led to my parent's bedroom. It had square bars for protection, but the last time I tried and successfully got through was when I was nine years old. I look like the very thief I was trying to avoid. But in reality, I was just trying to live. I got my head through the square and pushed my body to the side, then moved my shoulders diagonal and wiggled through. *I did it.*

The excitement died very fast. Now I was definitely paranoid. If I could do it, I know damn well a criminal could. The first thing I did was close and lock all the windows, closed the curtains, double-checked the doors, then went to my room. I got in bed and curled up into a ball. I set an alarm to go off in the next 1 hour and 30 minutes. That should be enough time to get my deserved sleep. Surprisingly, not even the stupid paranoia could hold off my sleep. Very soon, I was a goner.

It was nice. I mean the feeling of that relaxation soothing in, as tiredness moved out. Sleep truly is one of the best things ever. But of course, mine had to be short-lived. I didn't want my free day to go to waste. When I heard the alarm go off, I knew the journey had begun. I got out of bed and changed into something more sophisticated and comfortable. Something that would not cause suspicion when I'm out and about. I left the house through the same window I came in through and made sure no eyes were on me as I left our front yard. Taking a bike would cause too much trouble, so, walking would be more suitable. I started making my way to the town center, around the same place where Wesley and I met up to conduct our witness reports.

On my way there, I stopped at a small shop to buy myself a bar of dark chocolate. While there, I decided I wanted a pack of mint gum. I didn't want to buy it. So, I slipped it down the sleeve of my shirt and went to the counter to pay, you win some you lose some. I paid for my chocolate bar and left.

My next stop was a 2nd hand bookshop where books sold for a very cheap price. I decided to get myself a few volumes of Cowboy Bebop. With some money left to spare and not that many items on my to-buy-list, I went to the same coffee shop that Wesley and I visited the day of our witness reports. I got a seat next to the window that was facing Middleburg East, just across the road. I ordered coffee and a toasted cheese sandwich with an extra side plate. I placed my chocolate on that plate and proceeded to read, while taking sips of coffee and bites of my sandwich.

I was a paying customer, so there was no way they were kicking me out anytime soon. I sat and took my time because I had nothing better to do. So far, this was a better spent day than having to deal with Wesley and his little boy drama all day. I continued to read my manga, appreciating each word and each drawing. But then, something caught my eye. Movement in one of the windows facing the street. Movement coming from Middleburg East. I brushed it off, but there it was again. There were two figures holding each other From what it looked like, they were dancing hand in hand or doing some type of duo moves. I could tell by the height and weight differences that there were in fact two different people. *One of them* has to be Corey. They danced and they danced. I was mesmerised by what I was seeing. If that's him then this gives me hope. As much as I wanted to walk into that house and grab him, I didn't know what she was capable of. After a few minutes of me watching, the figures had gone. The movement had stopped and the house looked like it had always, for the past decades. It looked still. Now I was confused. I didn't know if what I saw was real, or if I was just crazy.

It has to be real. Well, it doesn't have to be, but I want it to be real. Whatever I saw would have to be put on hold until Friday when I can hopefully share these odd findings.

I brought my stay at the coffee shop to an end, packed away all my things, gave thanks to the workers and left. I decided to take a short walk around the park, not doing anything suspicious and just admiring all the nature and of the living things that have been given to us by who knows who. After looking and walking around, I soon got bored and walked into the thrift shop from where I get most of my clothes. I was familiar with the scene. Today wasn't a busy day. As such, most of the shops I went to were empty. I tried my luck with one employee who favours me. I picked out 1 black denim jacket and asked her; *"Hey Lara, do you think I can get this, no charge?"*

I was holding up the jacket.

"Kato, what are you doing here?" She paused and thought before asking, *"I know you have school. What's going on?"*

If I wanted this jacket, I couldn't pull off the *"You have no right to ask me"* sentence that I planned since morning. So, I tried to be nearly truthful, *"Just felt sick and didn't feel like going to school."*

"C'mon now. No lies. Here, I have a deal. Tell me the truth and you'll keep the jacket." She convinced.

I did what I had to do. I told her about everything that has been going on; excluding details about Kita and Corey and the whole investigation thing. I just told her that there was this boy I liked and we got into a fight about our other friend who had recently left us to join another group. The fight got so bad that I couldn't stand being at school.

"So, nobody knows where you are?" She asked quite concernedly.

"*Correct. Nobody does. I was just making my way back home though. I thought I'd stop by before that.*" I confirmed.

"*Little cheek. Well, a deal is a deal. We've been talking for quite a while, so you can take the jacket home with you.*" She smiled as she spoke.

"*Thank you so much Lara. This has by far made my week.*" I gripped the jacket firmer.

"*No problem, Kato, and I know this isn't my place, but give me a text when you are home and safe, ok?*" She said handing me a piece of paper with her telephone number written on it.

I took the paper; "*Jeez yeah, don't worry. I'll give you a text. Anyway, I'm off home now. See you around!*"

"*Bye, bye.*" She responded.

I took another glance at the paper. Her handwriting was quite neat. But I had no time to waste on that. So, I left the store and decided to take the long route home. This way would take me past the school and enable me to take my normal route home. I checked the time. It was quite early, but my sister along with my brother should be home around now. I started walking. I knew that if I was too late Wesley (if he cared), would notice me and try to talk to me. So, with that in mind, I went on in a hurry.

There wasn't much to do while walking home. I put on my earphones and started jamming to the beats playing in my ears. I wasn't happy today, despite the success. I still felt as if I've failed someone. I was of course unsure of who that person might be.

Maybe it was the tip I left the coffee shop worker.

Maybe it was the fact that I lied to Lara.

Maybe Wesley was waiting for me at school.

Maybe the clerk saw me take the gum from the store but was too tired to say anything.

Maybe my father was saving up this money but gave it to me because he felt sorry for me.

Maybe Corey saw me looking at him through the coffee shop window and danced faster so I would not notice that he's the one.

Maybe the bookshop cashier was disappointed because I took the last set of Cowboy Bebop. Maybe nothing. But, whatever way, it was a huge mess. Did I feel guilty about most of it?

No.

So, why then do I not feel satisfied?

This was surely not worth the thought, but could it get any worse?

When I arrived home, nobody was there. I realised I was too early, so I sat on the sidewalk waiting for them to arrive. It didn't feel safe, but I felt like I had walked forever, so taking a break seemed liable. With my head in my arms, I felt really sleepy.

Someone kicked me. I jerked up. I struggled to see who it was for a while. He kicked and kicked and kicked. Once my senses were activated, I noticed that it was Isaac. I got up and started chasing him around the street as my sister opened up the front door. When we retired home, I immediately knew my sister knew something was up. I wouldn't be surprised if she was following me all day.

"Hey sis, how was your day?" I said, trying to sound as casually as possible, without trying to hint that I had spent my day running around town.

"Well, my AP classes are really hard, so that's a total bummer. Other than that, why are you home early today?"

By the looks of it, she either had no clue about my whereabouts, or she was waiting for me to confess.

I have to respond anyway, *"Uh yeah. Well, the school let us out really early because they are having some sort of teacher meeting thing. So of course, my first thought was home."*

"Mhm, … they didn't notify anyone about your early return. But if that's the case, then we have a whole afternoon to do things!" She sounded excited.

"Yes! Sounds great, except I'm really tired." I responded.

I was tired and just wanted to go to bed … again.

"Well, I have something cut out for all three of us to do. It involves ice-cream!" You could tell from the drop of her voice that I killed her vibe.

I thought to myself that she sounded really excited. I couldn't let her down. *"You're paying though. I'm way too broke."* I reacted.

Isaac butted in while jumping up and down in excitement, *"B-b-but sis, I have soccer practice today."*

Holy crap, he does? This could be my way out.

"I've thought of that. We go to the food court first. Stop for a few bites, then we take you off to your soccer practice. Guys c'mon, don't worry, I got this." Kita outlined.

Yeah, she always does.

"I'm off to change then. Not going out in these same clothes." I turned and left.

While walking away, I heard Kita say under her breath, *"You've changed an awful lot today, Kato."*

I didn't realise what this meant until I got into my room. *She probably realised my change of clothes. She knows I didn't go to school. I'm going to die.*

eight was not helping me.

When I had changed, I sat on my bed, took out the paper Lara gave me and texted her that I had gotten home safely. I wasn't going to pull a Wesley and break another useful relationship. I took one last look at myself in the mirror and went back to my siblings. They were all ready. Soon, we left.

"Did you tell mom and dad that we'll be gone?" I asked.

"Yeah. I phoned to tell them and they were ok with it." She confirmed.

"Can we take our bikes?" Isaac asked as we walked out.

"Darn, I never thought about that. Yes, let's take our bikes." Kita answered.

We went to the back of the house and grabbed our bikes. Mine was black with purple stripes. Kita's was blue with black lining and Isaac's was green and pink. Colours didn't matter because we were happy to have them. After rolling them onto the street, we all got on and rode them towards the town centre. With Kita at the back and Isaac in the front, myself in the middle.

After minutes of riding, we arrived. We chained our bikes outside the small shop where I had bought the chocolate. As we walked, we passed all the shops I had visited just a few hours ago. We then arrived at the ice cream shop. When we entered, there was nobody inside but us and the cashier. We managed to score ourselves a discount because it was easier to convince someone for a discount when you are all alone.

I got a medium ice cream cup with milk chocolate chip cookies and cream along with lots of toppings. Kita got an ice cream cone with two scoops of strawberry and vanilla each.

Isaac got an ice cream cup with two milk chocolate scoops and toppings as well. We took a seat at the far end of the shop. As I sat to eat my ice cream, I looked all around the shop and admired the big colourful decorations of animated ice cream people in some type of weird universe where everything around them was candy and sweets. All this was good marketing and sure did keep anyone who entered very entertained.

As we made our way around eating the ice cream, we talked about casual sibling things. Television shows, favourite comic characters, etc. Nothing out of the ordinary. To us, it was a normal not-so-normal afternoon. We left the shop after thanking the worker and made our way back. Again, passing all the shops I had visited. This was filling me with some feeling of guilt, but as long as Kita didn't find out, I'm sure I will be fine.

When we located our bikes outside the store, Kita decided to use the leftover change from the ice cream to buy us some sweets. Isaac and I being grateful and excited, waited outside until she finished. Then, we hopped on our bikes and began to ride to the soccer club where Isaac would have his practice until 5.30 pm. Yes, that is a long wait, but it is something we would have to endure.

We arrived at the sports centre when his little mates were already on the field. We chained up our bikes and Isaac ran to his team. We followed him in no rush. Kita spoke to his coach and excused him for his late arrival. We sat on the grass on the field they were playing in and watched him practice. Yes, we judged how they played and how their coach instructed them, but with good intentions. It's just sibling love.

We had settled and gotten bored of watching young boys with big aspirations play. We sat back on the cold grass and that's when Kita broke into conversation,

"I know you didn't go to school today." She waited briefly.

There it is. I proceeded to let out a big sigh as she continued, *"I'm not some type of God, but the signs were everywhere... When I said take a break, this is not what I meant."*

I knew Kita knew. How couldn't she? I made up my mind to give the silent treatment and see what would happen next.

"Ok 'big boy'. Don't talk while I continue. It started in the morning when you asked dad for money - the asking wasn't wrong; it was the timing. You then waited for us to drive off while pretending to walk into school. Alas, did you forget rear view mirrors exist? I don't know where you went next, but I do know that at one point you came home. You got inside. Not through the front or back door because those were both locked, but through a window, your body could fit through."

She stopped to open up some sweets, and then continued,

"You then went around the house and closed all windows and curtains except the same window you came in through, which I'm guessing you again went out through. What made me suspect that something was wrong was when I saw you in different clothes. Then that stupid lie about school. Not to mention Lara told me she had seen you earlier. Which explains why you had an unbought jacket in your hands when you were sitting outside."

"Ok Kita, and? What do you want? It's not like I have to tell you everything that happens in my life." I bite back after she exposed me to no one but myself.

"Look, you're just a kid. You'll grow up. But until then, unless you want mom to find out and ban you from going out, you gotta listen to me." Her tone was firm and her face unmoved.

By the look of things, she was enjoying seeing defeat. This saw me have no choice but to speak to her.

"All that happened today was me taking some time away from school. Nothing big really. I went to the coffee shop and the bookshop and to the thrift shop. I didn't get in any type of trouble nor did I get hurt. I swear it's not a big deal." I tried my way out.

As much as I wanted to be defensive, I knew she was right. If my parents knew, I wouldn't be able to leave the house for a while. Blackmail? I didn't really know, but I had no choice.

"Great now that it's been confirmed. No more slacking off. Unfortunately, if you do again, I cannot let you go on with your investigations. A repeat would just show me you can't be responsible." She bossed.

"Man, just calm down. You saying that just means you don't care about what we're doing." I tried the emotional approach.

"That's right. I value your future more. Plus, I'm pretty sure I've been the one helping you out more than your little sessions with Wesley." She told me outrightly.

She was right. It bothered me. She knew I needed her. So now, all my blunders were to her advantage. Although her talk was for the right reasons, it didn't sit right with me. I thought I would have the upper hand throughout, Nevertheless, it had been taken from me.

I guess since I am powerless, I am forced to follow the rules or next time, I'd just play it out more carefully. She has a good eye and if I was to compete, I'd have to match that.

We went the rest of Isaac's practice not speaking to each other. It wasn't as awkward as I expected though. This incident took me back to before we started talking. For the rest of the time, there wasn't that much interaction between my sister and me. The only noise between us was the constant chewing of sweets and ruffling of sweet packets, along with the little kids shouting out on the field and their coaches getting frustrated.

When Isaac had finished his training, we handed him his share of the sweets. Cleaned up our surrounding area, then made our way to our bikes. We got on, waited for one another and began our ride.

It was getting cold and the streets were alive. We had to be careful in the way we made our rounds. Cars were everywhere and most human drivers didn't really care. When we arrived home, the lights were on and the smell of dinner reached us before we even stepped in. My mother had just finished preparing the lovely meal and as always, before we could touch or taste it, we had to clean ourselves up. I quickly showered, then changed into my usual comfy fit. I looked around my room and the memories of my adventures came rushing back to me. It felt like my adventure took place a day before it actually did. Now I had to sit down at a family dinner and hold the guilt of what I had done.

"So, guys, how was it? Kita told me about the fun things she had planned." Said mother.

"Well mommy, we had a good time. We went for ice cream, then rode all the way to my soccer practice." Isaac responded.

"Yeah, it went well for me as well. The ice cream was good." I said, laughing and trying to up the mood.

Kita however didn't say much. For the rest of dinner, Isaac went blabbing about his practice and his team and whatever seemed relevant to him. Listening to this soon got me bored.

After I finished, I made it a mission that I do my evening chores the fastest I had ever for two reasons; to avoid talking to Kita and to get to sleep as soon as possible. All of these were enough motivation to keep my body active for a little longer. Despite all the efforts, I still ended up alone in the kitchen with my sister. We both did our chores in silence. Looking back at how much our relationship has grown and the memories we have in this kitchen really made me feel bad. I didn't exactly regret going out, but I did regret her finding out. I wasn't in the mood to talk. We each kind of just did what we did, without acknowledging one another.

Luckily, I managed to finish up before her so. I left the kitchen and was going to my room when she called out; *"Good night, Kato. Sleep tight."*

"Thanks. You too Kita." I felt bad leaving her there alone.

I didn't expect her to still wish me off well after our recent encounter, but I was grateful she did. As I entered my room, I got into bed and checked my phone. There was a single text from Lara. It was just a bunch of words saying that she was happy I was home safe and blah, blah. I couldn't care less because tomorrow I had to go to school and I was not looking forward to it.

When I woke up, I didn't want to go to school, but after these past days, I knew it wasn't about what I wanted.

I took my time. I made a special effort to actually eat some breakfast.

I made a bowl of cereal and a cup of coffee. Seeing as no one else was out of their rooms, I sat down and watched the news. Watching the news all day could make a person really depressed. Most of the reports are filled with the horrible things in the world. When they do report on something 'good' it's usually irrelevant, like a new star in space. As I watched the morning news show, the female presenter definitely caught my eye. She was so pretty. Her eyebrows were perfect. Her nose was a masterpiece. Her hair was bright red and her lips a soft pink. Her outfit (although I couldn't see it all), was formal and suited to fit her exceptionally well. God has his favourites. I kept saying as I packed and cleaned away my dishes.

The house was waking up and everybody was preparing to start their day. Since I had everything set, I went outside, sat down on the sidewalk in the exact place I did yesterday and waited for the family to get ready.

I greeted Kita when she got out of the house and she thankfully greeted me back. She seemed happy today. I was glad that the past was left where it was meant to be left and that this day had been off to a good start. We got into the car and made our journey to school.

I was still reading the Cowboy Bebop I got yesterday, so that was my entertainment. When we got to school, I knew Kita made an effort not to let me slip behind their backs again. I know that she kept a keen eye on me as I actually walked into the school building. Right.

The stench of high-schoolers I had managed to dodge off for just a day was back. As I passed them one by one, the worry I had for Wesley increased.

Kato, notice how Wesley didn't show up at your house after your absence from school. eight reminded me.

Until now I never thought about that. At this moment, it's all I could think about.

Meanwhile, you went to check up on him. This shows you how much he doesn't care.

No, eight, it shows how much I care.

Yes. Sure, hurts that he couldn't be bothered but now that I've come to this realisation, I couldn't be bothered either.

You can't have the same person twice. It's so unlucky for him. He gives me a new Wesley and I'll sure as hell give him a new Kato.

That's right. I made a new commitment to eight. I mean, to myself: ***Think twice before committing to someone who does not appreciate you.***

I stopped in mid-walk when I saw Wesley sitting in the exact place doing the same thing, he does every other morning. I decided I was not going to fall into tradition. I'd rather wait in the bathrooms until the bell calling for first-class rings.

Was I chickening out?

Not exactly. I just wanted time to think over and perfect who I wanted this new Kato to be.

Would he be charming?

Would he be cold?

Would he be carefree?

It was hard to decide who I wanted to be. The above all sounded good because of the multiple fantasies I've formed in my head. No matter which I become, each of them would be secretly robbing the current Kato of something. I wasn't so sure of what yet. It feels like it would be fun to try these out, but unfortunately, I'm not a very good actor. I was running out of time because very soon, I would be in the first class of the day, seated right next to him.

Charming Kato was the one I finally decided to become. I admit, I was under pressure and the bell had rung, so in all the best fantasies I created, *charming* had won.

I waited till the hallways were quiet, then I sprinted off to class. All to make it seem like I was actually late for school, and not avoiding his presence. I slowed down when I neared the class and perfected this new persona. I walked into the class, excused myself and sat down right next to Wesley. I saw him out of the corner of my eye watching me as I didn't acknowledge his presence. I fumbled in my bag for a scrawny notebook. I then looked up in my best charming face and said, *"Good morning, Wesley."*

His movement was predicted. He pretended that just seconds before he was not looking at me, and responded shyly, *"Good morning, Kato, nice to see you after all this time."*

I obviously knew our relationship was tarnished and it would take a lot of work to get us both back into our comfort zones. At least, I also knew that none of this was my fault and if he didn't apologise, then things were never going back.

"Yeah, nice to see you too." I said as I pretended to follow along with the class.

This class was a drag although I was happy that the whole charming persona was going well. At one point in the class, I took a break and just stared at Wesley. It must have been for a few minutes. I was pleased to see that he was getting uncomfortable. He didn't want to look my way. He was increasing his writing pace and fiddling with his fingers.

When the first class was over, it came time for the second period. The second period was art. Our art class was our most interactive and my favourite one. We only have art twice a week for an hour, meaning our class didn't get enough time to finish projects. As such, projects often had to be done at home.

I entered the art class and had a brief conversation with my teacher about an art piece due after half-term. She had agreed to let me take it home from next week, so I could get it done. After that, I went over to Wesley. While focusing on my project, I stroke a conversation, *"So, you missed me yesterday?"*

"Yeah, a little bit. School was boring and I had no one to talk to. It was really hard." He too focused on his project.

Our art topic for this term was interdimensional. We could explore all types of visual art forms provided by the school. Wesley's project was colourful, he was making an art piece consisting of several squares all in a row, leading into a narrowed eye at the overall centre. Each square had an individual colour which would make your eyes hurt if you stared at it long enough.

"I was meaning to ask you where on earth were you? I came down there to check up on you, but when I arrived at around 4.05:13 pm, nobody was home so, I figured maybe something bigger than me happened." He laughed it off.

I was wrong. Well, I wasn't really wrong because I had no idea. eight said.

Shut up eight. Let me think.

eight was wrong. Wesley did try to check up on me. Which now means that I could drop this stupid persona; which I never really liked anyway, and ease the slight grudge I may or may not have had on Wesley.

"Well, you see, uh yeah yesterday was a really complicated day. If I had to go through everything then we'd surely be stuck in this conversation all day." I could finally relax back into my original persona.

"Pleep ploop. No need. Just glad you're ok." He stopped what he was doing and made some conversational intimacy happen. *"Look I wanted to apologise for what I did earlier this week. What I did wasn't a good gesture and I know you had the correct intentions, so, I'm really sorry for the havoc I caused."*

I too stopped what I had been doing, took in his apology and thought up a response. *"It's great that you've come to terms with what has happened. I accept your apology. Also, this is an invitation to meet me at my house tomorrow after school, to you know ... talk about the things regarding Corey."*

I totally nailed the response by biting back with something casual to beat off just how cold it actually was.

"Sheesh yes, I-I can, I can do that." He sounded timid.

Great! Now that this whole mess has been solved, I can try to function and think normally. It's crazy to think that I let my guard down these past few days for some 15-year-old; although he still does mean a lot to me. #neveragain.

Following our resolution, we went on with our day as usual. By the end of the school day, I was certain that our relationship was fixed. On the way home, I was more than happy. I plugged in my earphones and played some tunes. I looked back at how ignorant I was and how I overreacted to some stupid ripple in the way things are. Next time it has been agreed upon that I should probably listen to Kita because she seems to actually know what's best for me.

I got home and I was joyous. I did my routine with more motivation as I was looking forward to my after-dinner conversation with my sister. I couldn't wait to tell her about how she was right and that we kind of needed to sort things out before Friday. The first part will definitely boost her ego (which I didn't like). I'm doing it because I'm starting not to care about ego, and starting to enjoy having the bond we have.

I did all my homework and changed into my usual fit. I sat down on my bed just reading, waiting for my name to be called.

"*Kato, food is ready!*" Mother shouted.

And off I went.

I reached the table and had a good-ish dinner. I was not a huge fan of stir-fry, so that brought down my mood a little bit.

But at last, the ending of dinner had arrived. I did my chores and sat in my regular spot waiting for Kita to hurry up. When she came and sat down, she started the conversation as always,

"So, my main man Kato, how was school?"

Every time she started the conversation, she made it sound like we do not live in the same house and do not see each other every day. But hey, that's beside the point. I told her about my whole scene in the morning. About the bathrooms and added a little comedy to make her laugh.

It worked.

Kita laughed really hard. She made a lot of eye contact as she laughed. I told her about the whole persona nonsense as well - You could say I was being an open book. I then went on to tell her about our conversation in class one and about the things I noticed. I told her about art class. This seemed to have been her favourite part. I mean who doesn't like a 'cute' resolution?

I told her everything about the rest of my day and it felt like I was the narrator of a movie. I think that my storytelling skill are improving. Especially when talking to Kita, because I do not want to keep her both guessing and suspicious.

"Jesus, Kato. Your life is hectic. To be honest, this could never be me. I knew you and Wesley would sort things out. I'm happy my advice helped. " She was bare.

"Yeah... Thanks Kita. It may not seem like it, but you help me a lot." I was a little embarrassed.

She can't know how much I cherish her. I mean if she does find out, I'll die.

"Well, I mean, not that I'm assuming anything, but do you like Wesley?" She spoke again.

What was with this question eight?

"B-U-No wha-what makes you think so? You know what? I don't even wanna hear it because it is false." I stuttered.

I know. But that question came as a shock. Kita can't go around saying such.

"Man, I knew you weren't ready to hear that question. It's ok. You're freaking out and I respect you, so I won't ask again". She blocked me.

"I demand a new subject which is tomorrow's meeting with Wesley. I think we could just neaten the house up a bit and prep some information. By prep some information, I mean like write down those findings you spoke to me about the other night." I suggested.

"It can be done. But why are we trying so hard to impress Wesley? If he comes in here and we don't have anything done, I'm sure he'll appreciate it." Kita was also a straight talker.

"Yes and no. I've been over to his place and compared to ours, he is a man of high standards. They even have a computer with the Internet... I know I may be trying hard, but he's probably

the first friend I'm bringing over and I'm nervous." I tried to convince my own sister.

"Nervous?" She rolled her eyes, *"I'll help you alright, but I need you to show some gratitude as well."* She blackmailed me ..., or tried to.

"What do you mean by gratitude?" I questioned.

"When was the last time you spoke to me and asked me how I was doing? Or about my day? My relationships? Now I don't expect you to that this every day, but some amount of interest in my life would be cool." My sister sounded desperate.

Oh yeah, she has a life (not in a rude way), but she was completely right again.

"Shoot I'm sorry Kita...there is no excuse for what I have done, so I'm just really sorry. I've been really self-absorbed lately, but it will start changing, I promise!" I told her.

"No need for an apology, but I do greatly appreciate that. Anyway, run off to bed now. It's quite late." She ordered me ... as always.

"Good night, Kita." I gave her a hug.

"Good night." She hugged back.

That was cute. The sibling bond was amazing. The feeling is fulfilling too.

Friday the 1st of June.

I got out of bed and prepared for school. Got out, had breakfast while watching the morning news lady, then got into the car.

I arrived at school and made my way in. I saw Wesley and did my little scare. It always works. We had a conversation about today, just; confirming time and everything.

I wasn't expecting anything major to happen today, so when I got called to the principal's office, I just thought I had forgotten something.

I left class and through the hallways, I walked. When I entered the reception, there was nobody in the waiting room - I started to panic a little.

"Huh, good morning, ma'am. I was called to the office?" I said, addressing the receptionist.

"Ok. Are you Kato Sterik?" She confirmed.

"Yes." I replied.

"Ok. Make your way to the principal please." She led her right hand to the principal's door, pointing specifically with her forefinger.

Crap I might actually be in trouble. I thought as I entered the office.

When I walked in, there they were. Two police officers and my principal, all sitting down.

"Good morning, Kato." My principal addressed me. *"Take a seat."* He rushed me to an empty chair.

I sat down calmly.

"Here with me today are officers Nason and Groth. They are one of the many officers working on Corey's case." He explained.

eight, isn't this intense!

I didn't say anything, but I nervously look at their uniform, handcuffs and guns.

Noticing my body language, one of the officers said, *"Kato, you are not in trouble. We just need to ask you a few questions regarding his case."* He signalled to the principal to leave.

He did so.

"Ok sir." I said.

My hands were shaking.

"Ok then let's begin." He placed sometime of recording device and the desk.

"My name is Officer Groth. Here with me is my partner; Officer Nason. We are from the Middleburg Police department, here to ask you a few questions. Do we have your permission to record?"

"Yes sir." How on earth could I refuse?

Officer Groth paused. He made eye contact with officer Nason and then continued.

"We shall now begin. Was Corey in distress or in fear of something before his disappearance?"

"No." I answered.

Immediately after I spoke, Officer Nason wrote something in his notebook.

"Was Corey in contact with anyone before his disappearance?" Officer Groth asked.

I thought that the police had found the letters. If they have, why were they asking me something they already knew?

"Yes." I confirmed. Officer Nason wrote more.

"Who?" Officer Groth continued.

"I don't know her name, age, description or how they met. All I know is that she attends Meek High. I'm not even sure if she is real." I responded.

"Tell us more about their relationship?" Officer Nason spoke.

"Well, they communicated through letters which I found very weird. They were making plans to meet during the weekend. I think there might have been romantic intentions between them. I don't know for sure." I detailed, without really having any details.

"Anything else?" Officer Groth asked.

"Corey didn't tell us much about their relationship. Only small things you know." I said.

"Us?" The officer questioned.

"Uh yes, my friend Wesley and I."

"Ok". Officer Groth responded, while officer Nason continued to take notes.

"Here are three different letters. We would like you to choose which one you think is real."

Officer Groth said, putting the letters down on the table.

So, they do know?

eight has left me ... or so it seemed.

I took a moment to observe the letters, taking note of the dates they were sent on, the contents and the stamps. After a few minutes, I gave my answer to the police.

"Thank you, Kato, for your cooperation." Officer Groth said.

"We are finished with questioning. But if you have any new information pop down to the station. If we feel the need to obtain extra information, we will be in touch with your guardian. You are free to leave." He concluded.

"Ok, thank you." I bowed and walked away.

I met the principal outside and mumbled a quick goodbye.

When I was walking back to class, I heard on the intercom calling that it was Wesley's turn.

I continued walking down the hallways.

I met Wesley walking in the direction of the office. So, before I returned to class, I stopped him and said,

"Don't worry about what's going on in there, just stay calm." I walked off.

The rest of the day whisked by so fast. Lesson after lesson, we learned. Conversation after conversation, we spoke. Foot in front of foot, we walked. Word after word, we wrote. Minute after minute, time passed.

When the last bell rang, we packed our stuff up and waited on one another before walking.

This walk was peaceful and we stood really close to each other, sharing one side each of my earphones. We were slowly bobbing our heads to the music and maintaining the same walking speed. In almost no time, we had arrived home.

Before opening the front door, I immediately became insecure of my own home.

"Hey, a quick note before we go in. My house isn't big or fancy." I cautioned.

"Look, a house is a house. I'm not one to judge." Wesley said

It had a musk and the interior design wasn't exactly the best. Nonetheless, I had to suck it all in because there was nothing that could be changed in the moments of me opening the front door.

When I stepped into the house, I was taken aback (only a little), at how neat it was. I obviously didn't clean it up, meaning Kita did. The house's interior was still crappy, but everything else was cool. The rooms were neat, and the musk was faint and filled with other smells like cleaning supplies hiding in between perfume. I put my bag down and took out all the things I needed, then indicated for Wesley to do the same. When he had finished, I showed him my colourful room and informed him that he should feel welcome. He gave the usual compliments that people would give and me being unsure if he was telling the truth brushed it off. I told Wesley I was going to grab some stuff and I'd be back. I dashed out of the room.

I went to the kitchen to fetch some snacks. On my way back, I checked for Kita, but she was not in her room.

I returned to mine and nearly dropped what I was holding when I saw her sitting on my chair. She seemed to be having a conversation with Wesley. I laid down the snacks on the floor and began the so-called meeting,

"Good afternoon, all, welcome to the first official meeting of the F.C. I hope that we can put our minds together and solve this case."

"Uh yes...hi? Kato. What does F.C. mean?" Asked Kita.

"Oh, it stands for Find Corey. It's rather basic, but it's something I thought we could stick to unless, of course, someone has a better idea. I don't really mind." I clarified.

"Nah I think it's ok. Anyway, we got a long way to go, so shall we start?" Wesley spoke.

"Uh well, yes we can." I looked at Kita as I explained that, *"Kita has some information that I found extremely useful to our overall plan. So, she and I have been doing some digging by*

ourselves and on Monday evening, we found this." I handed
Wesley a folder that had everything Kita said that evening. It
was well written down. I stayed up a little longer than usual,
writing this down last night.

"*We'll give you a minute to take it in.*" I told.

As Wesley read through the papers Kita and I just sat
trying not to look awkward and tired. I studied Wesley's
facial expression as he read through this all.

"*Well done, Kita. I think this is the most valuable
information we've gotten since this whole thing. I mean Kato
and I set the foundation, but you certainly brought it up. I like
your line of thinking about the cult or group of people because
earlier on this week, I had the same idea. It has to be a group of
people. But I did research using the computer I have at home
and at the school library about cults and sects. I discovered
things that quickly threw me off the whole idea.*"

Wesley got out his own file and handed it to Kita. I shifted
around to get next to her and to read what she was reading.
While we did so Wesley continued,

"*Cult activity revolves around vulnerable people abiding
by one leader's rules. The leader often practices things that
go beyond modern beliefs of practising unusual religions,
spiritual, or philosophical beliefs, and all that. The town folk of
Middleburg have shown no major signs of cult activity. Which
is a good sign. Along with cult activity, I am sure that they*

would sacrifice more than just one adolescent boy every four years. Of course, it depends on their practice, but it is highly unlikely nonetheless."

"So that leaves us with our original suspicion. Ms Murry." I said, trying to sound helpful.

"While I was out on Wednesday, I went to the coffee shop facing towards the home. ... I saw movement through the windows. When I looked carefully, I noticed two people or figures that looked like humans. I'm sure they were doing some type of ballroom dancing because they had synchronised movement. Call me crazy, but I think it was Corey up there." I disclosed.

I knew that what I said had come at the wrong time by seeing their reactions. They stayed seated and looked at me like I was crazy. I know it's weird, but I saw what I saw. I can't lie about this stuff.

"Kato, are you sure?" Kita broke the silence, much to my relief.

"Yeah, are you sure? What you're saying isn't a joke. It could give us all false hope." Wesley added.

"Guys, I swear. I won't lie. Not at a time like this. All you gotta do is trust me." I tried to convince them.

"We do trust you Kato. Our next plan is probably going to be our biggest." Said Kita swiftly, moving on to what we were all waiting for.

"We need to plan our break-in. This is something that has to be done with extra caution. We could all lose our lives." She looked intense.

"But not all of us have to go." I assured them.

Kita continued,

"Correct. We'll deep dive into all of that when we've figured out our way around the house and how this will all work. We've got the layout of the house, which includes all the different rooms and hallways, etc. but what we need now is to rule out possibilities. I mean possibilities of messing up. We just need to get Corey and leave. After that is done, we can now go ahead and inform the police." Kita had taken the leadership role from both of our hands.

"But none of us have ever stepped foot inside the house. With a total of 21 rooms in the house, it would be a lot to search." I shared my concern.

"No kidding, but we can't do anything about it". Kita pointed at the blueprints, *"You two are going to be the ones going in."* She instructed.

"Wait! Why us?" Wesley freaked out, giving me a look that suggested that he did not trust me anymore.

"That's because somebody gotta be on the lookout and if I'm being honest, I'm the only person I trust for the job. Anyway, back to the plan. You'll most likely enter from the bottom up, so it eases suspicion. You will most likely enter from a door

in the barn. Ms Murry has no idea that you guys are in her house, so you have to be stealthy. There is a trap door leading into the basement." She pointed at a hatched look entry and continued.

"*Once you get into the basement, you don't know what to expect, but if it happens to be too dangerous, climb back up. From the basement, you'll then climb a set of stairs leading you to the first-floor hallway. You'll take your first right and look for this doorway that leads to the kitchen. From there, I want you to go through to the living room which is this big area over here-*'"

At this, she grabbed four markers from my desk. I assumed it was four markers for the four levels of the home; basement, first floor, second floor and attic. How the layout on our paper was quite confusing since the home had levels. Each level had to be included separately. The marking of where you'd leave one and enter the other was marked down. So was the name of each level.

Below is the layout of our map. It will give you a better idea of what Kita is going on about. Good luck in interpreting it.

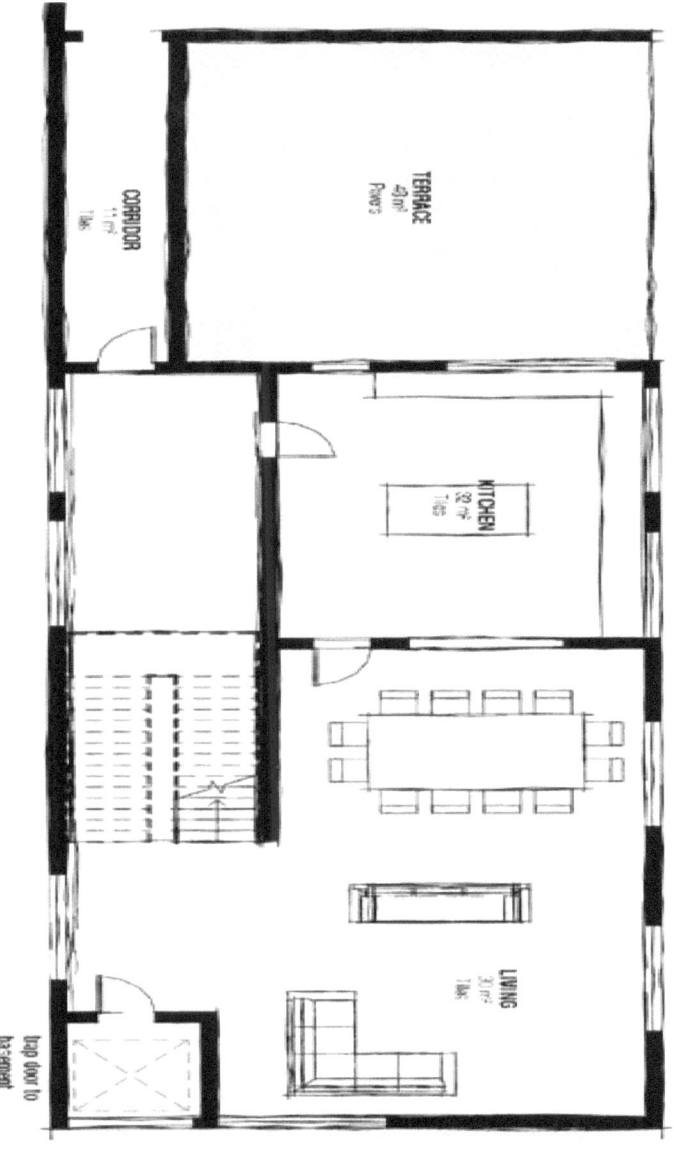

FIRST FLOOR

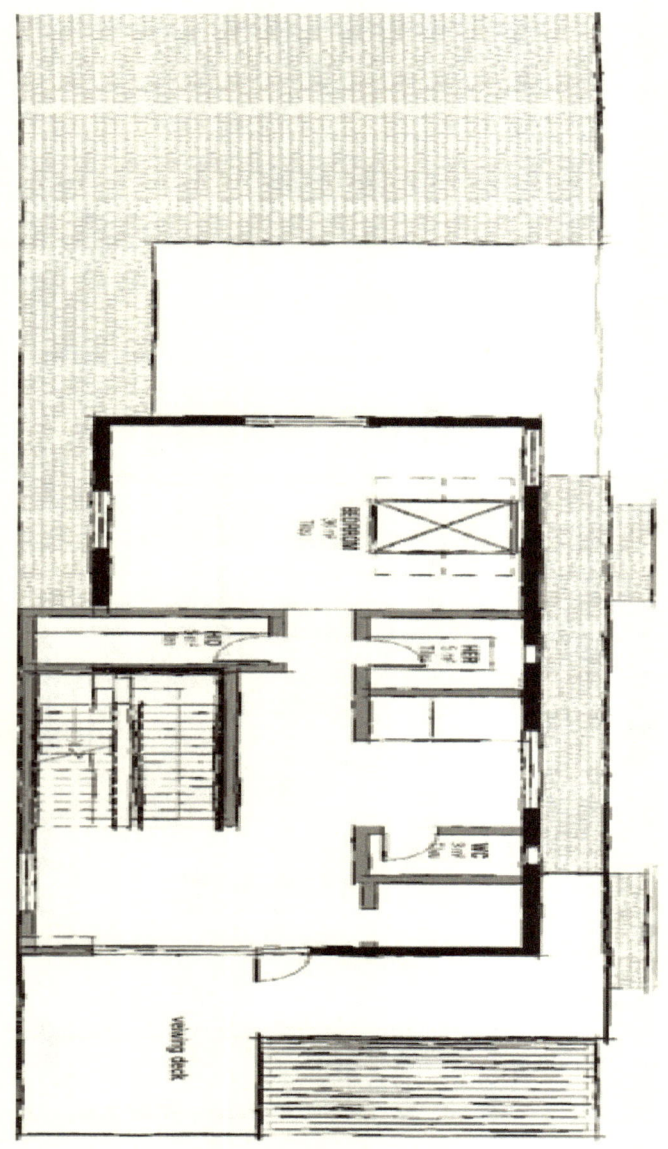

SECOND FLOOR

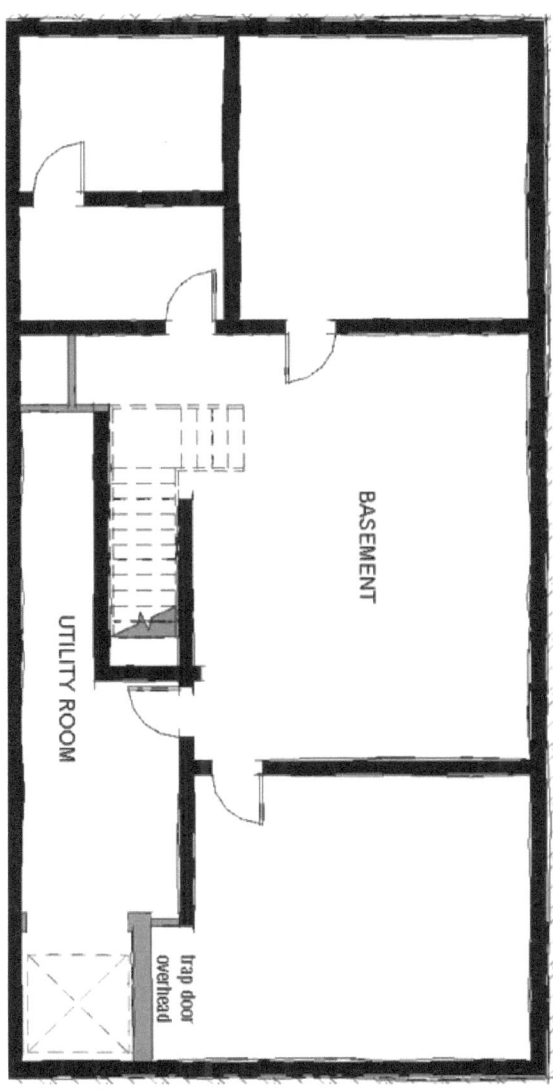

BASEMENT

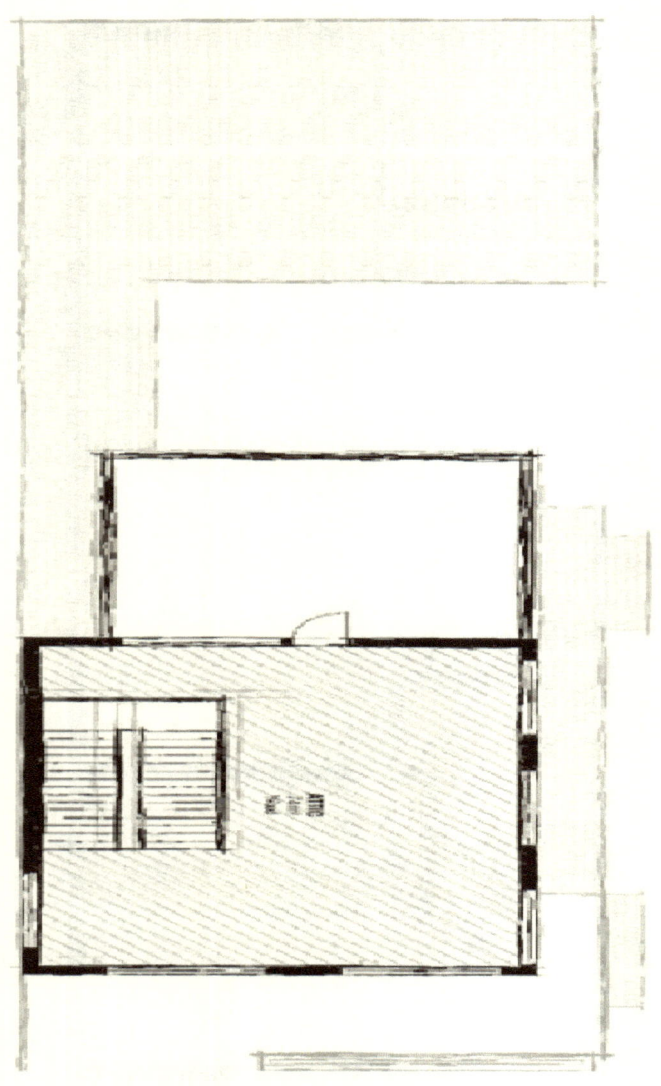

ATTIC

We watched as Kita drew our path lines, making sure we crossed every room and not a spot was missed. She explained to us how it is very unlikely that Corey would be on the first floor because of how hard it would be to restrain him and that he would most likely be on the other three floors. Even so, we should always be on high alert.

"I've seen Corey's build and I know he wouldn't have been easy to restrain. It's a possibility that she has other ways of capturing the boys. If that is the case, you boys aren't going in that house without air filtering masks." My sister stopped.

I was filled with admiration for her.

"Why would we need those?" Asked Wesley.

"Drugs." She said plainly.

"Drugs?" I felt shivers.

"Yes. In science, we were talking about this drug that has surfaced in South America. It wipes your mind blank and makes it easy for a person to control you. However, you will regain your memories according to the dose given. Regardless, this is one of the most harmful drugs to exist. It's hard to track the things going in and out of this country, so we don't know for sure who has this and how they are using it. Now, I may be talking bullshit, but I don't think I've gotten anything wrong since I joined FC." Kita took the time to talk.

"What's the drug called?" I asked. Surprised that Kita did not mention this to me during our numerous talks at home … But focus!

"Ah yes, I forgot to say. It's called scopolamine. Remember that. It affects you when inhaled. Hence, I need you to wear air filtering masks." She explained.

"Where do we get this mask from?" Wesley inquired.

"We have some in our science lab, so I'll pull a few strings and get them out the day before we operate." She fake-smiled for the first time since she started talking.

"When will this be?" Wesley was curious.

"Well, since we run on the same school calendar, we'll go during mid-term. Mid-term is a whole week from the 18th to the 22nd. If you look at it in days, we have nine days, since school closes on Friday the 15th and opens on Monday the 25th. Our venture will be during the week … at the most unsuspecting times of the day." Kita explained patiently.

"Ok, so we've gotten down everything we need to do. Now what's next is making sure we're bulletproof - not literally, because I'm sure it's expensive. Like preparing masks, clothing, learning our way and mastering the routes, finding quick ways to escape and how it's going to work if we need the police or SOS backup." Said Wesley.

This sounded scary, but we were all determined. We would do it for Corey, but for each of us.

We spoke about all that he mentioned. Masks will be brought by Kita. We will find all the suitable clothing at the clothing shop where Lara works at. We would need to go over the routes every day before the operation and we will take the map in with us in case.

We spent more time going over this. We marked escape routes at every floor we were going at and finally, the police SOS was quite simple. We would be taking our phones in with us. Since Kita would be waiting outside for us to return and if we needed an SOS, all we needed to do was text her the letters SOS and she would know immediately to phone the police.

I was feeling really confident and happy that Corey might be free soon, although, I found it strange that a person would hold a human being captive for so long without killing or disposing of their body even though by now, it had become clear that everybody has different preferences, or should I say fetishes.

"So, the police came to interview us today." I said to Kita since it wasn't mentioned. But also, as a way to urge her to intensify our plan.

"Wait, really?" She asked. *"You guys never mentioned anything."* She added, running her eyes between Wesley and I.

"I don't know ..." I attempted to respond.

"So, tell me how it went then!" She semi-shouted.

"They just asked a bunch of questions, then presented me with three types of letters, like you mentioned, and asked me to identify which one I thought was real. I don't know about Wesley though. We have not talked about it yet." I concluded from my side.

"It was the same for me." Wesley added before I continued

"I was so nervous, thinking about the interview. It doesn't have an impact on our investigation anymore. We've come to a suspect, so doesn't this mean that we can drop the letter talk?" I made sense, hoping that the others would agree.

"That is partly true. I wonder where the police are in their investigation?" Wesley added.

"Whatever I agree with you both, but since we've solved this problem, this meeting is adjourned!" Kita said.

While waiting for his parents to arrive, Wesley ended up having dinner with us and then joined us in the living room in front of the TV. We eat dessert together while attempting to watch a movie.

Not that long into the movie, his parents arrived.

Wesley thanked my parents for letting him stay and giving him meals. He then grabbed his stuff and we went out together.

I greeted his parents and thanked them for allowing Wesley over.

I wished them well.

I gave Wesley a hug and waited for them to drive off before going back inside.

Once inside I sat down and continued to watch the movie. I never really sat down with my family in moments like this, but I swore to myself that I would make an effort to get as close to them in these next few days because just like everyone else in the F.C. group, we were unsure of whether we would make it out of that house alive or not. Although this is my original idea in the first place, it seems that I've lost all the confidence that I had started off with. But no matter how much confidence I lose going through the process, I swore to myself again that I would not back out of going into Middleburg East and trying my best to free Corey.

When the movie was over, we all cleaned up our spaces and went to our rooms. While I was in my room, I began to look around, checking if there was something I had to do before going to sleep. As I continued to search, I remembered that I had forgotten to say 'Thank you' to Kita. So, without a second thought, I jumped out of bed and went to her room. When I got to the door, I knocked then entered. When I got in, I saw that she was sitting at her desk doing her homework.

She's a really good child.

All she said when I entered was; ... *"Yes Kato?"*

She didn't look up at me or acknowledge my presence in a better way. I understood since I was bothering her. For a brief moment, I thought that I should put more effort into my schoolwork. But then, I remembered that I've tried before and it's ok that I have different values; at least I think so.

Kita is in her final year, while I have just entered high school. It must be tough having so many things on your mind, but I knew she would make it work. She always does.

"Hey sis, I'm sorry for disturbing you while you do your work. So, I'll make it quick. I am extremely grateful and thankful for all you did today; cleaning up and contributing to this whole thing. You mean a lot to me and I hope that one day, once this has all blown over, I can pay you back." I felt like I was giving a short speech to a brick wall.

She gave a faint smile. I knew she was tired. Who wouldn't be? I felt sorry for her, even though it's hard to imagine that she also goes through hardships. I guess I find it hard to sympathise with anyone in general.

"Do you plan to pay in cash or card?" She asked jokingly.

"Well, seeing as I'm broke at the moment, I'll think up a contract which allows me to pay without using such means." I answered back by playing along.

I gave her the last hug of the day and even a little kiss on the cheek and retreated to my room.

As I lay in my bed, I kept on thinking about today's meeting. The pros and cons of FC. Everything was coming into place, but I could still feel a part of me who didn't want to do any of this. It was risky and I guess losing one life is better than three. So, why don't we leave this for the police? But I also knew that if I didn't act now, I would carry the guilt of a dead body on my hands and I would never be able to shake it off. I was torn between dying and living with death. Nothing could be worse. With under two weeks to put our plans to action, I had to choose fast.

When I woke up on Saturday, I knew how I wanted to spend my weekend. Instead of doing something worthwhile, I was going to do nothing at all. I was going to avoid trouble by doing all my chores and staying in my room, leaving only to get food. It sounded like a plan. I didn't have the energy to go out and about because the week I had was my most tiring. I liked the idea of relaxing for a while and regaining all the strength, much needed for the weeks ahead.

Saturday was extremely successful. I didn't do anything but clean up and lazy around. I stayed in my room for the most part of my day. I drew pictures, listened to music, read books and acted out some scenes, took spontaneous naps and snuck out for snacks. Nobody seemed to care, so I was not bothered. Everyone was doing their own things and living their lives.

"Today even our clocks are not made of clockwork - so why should our world be?" Ian Stewart.

I know the above quotation means millions of things to millions of people, but I chose to see it as Stewart telling us that we should not bound by the concept of time.

Although you think that I may be using it in the wrong sense, I think that wasting my day is sort of a protest, ... saying that I do not have to be active in order to be fulfilled.

My Saturday agrees with Benjamin Disraeli that, *"Duty does not exist without faith."*

Right now, I have no faith. Therefore, I cannot fulfil my duty of being a good older/younger brother to my siblings or a good son to my parents or even a good friend to Corey and Wesley.

I think that I deserve rest. That I deserve to do nothing for a day, or maybe even two. I am not self-fish because I saw in my mother's women's magazine that there's a new thing called 'self-care' and it's becoming more common. But imagine if everyone in the world took rest for one day ... it will be different outcomes for different people. But the world wouldn't be the same.

At the dinner table that night, my blood boiled as my family were having a conversation. Isaac asked my parents why people have children and for what reason.

My mother, who was definitely confident in her words stated clearly;

"Well, you see, a family is structured much like a workplace – the family unit being the company. The father acts as the head or owner of the company. The mother as employee number one, or the company manager and the children are workers, specifically labourers, who are answerable to the mother and father, but mostly answerable to the mother, who in turn reports to the head or owner ... father. The head of this workplace or father is meant to make sure everybody gets fed and is healthy but also performs their duties. Employee number one or the mother makes sure everyone is happy and fulfilling their duties according to how they have been duly taught by both the company owner and employee number one. As days progress, the labourers are mostly taught values acceptable to the company owner and lesser so, the manager. For this reason, both the manager and the labourers are workers who are there to work and receive the benefits of work in terms of the luxuries provided by the company owner and subsequently in form of inheritance."

Her tone didn't change. Her posture didn't change. Her facial expression didn't change. My mother knew the impact of her words and it felt like she was saying this to prove a point or to prove how superior she and my father are. Kita and I looked at each other. We could feel the discomfort in what she had said. We continued to stare at her as she explained on and on about how children are meant to be workers. She explained how they grow into adolescence with experience and how by adulthood, they are positioning themselves to become company owners and managers with levels of ease as determined by how morally, socially and culturally well the manager has empowered them and academically and financially through what inheritance the company owner left for them.

Not changing her opinion once in what she had said.

My father sat quietly at the other end of the table. He did not add anything to this. He just ate as if nothing out of the ordinary had happened.

This isn't unusual for my dad. He is a really quiet person but when he was angry, he stripped everyone of their right to an opinion. Most of the time, I would think that my father is afraid of my mother because of how we fear her. She uses her place in the hierarchy to assert her dominance in beatings, which when serious would leave marks such as lines or bruises. In this conversation, my father knew that if he was to disagree, they would argue all night long and if he was to agree, my mother would use it to her advantage. Wisely as I sensed, he chose silence to preserve peace.

I did not want to be around such a toxic environment, so without a word, I left the table and went to do the dishes. While doing them - eight and I had a conversation.

Is mother crazy?

No eight, she's just being her normal self.

It's scary, isn't it? Imagine if all parents thought like that.

Well, mother doesn't know that every parent has different reasons for having children and each family is different. Like I'm sure Wesley's parents feel different about their family environment after losing a child.

Same. She looked so smug while she was saying it. I wanted to punch her.

If you punched, I would've gotten in trouble and not you, you idiot! I'm glad you didn't do anything.

Well, we haven't been doing anything all day, so, I just followed your lead and kept these hands to themselves.

That was an excellent move. Now, please, I need to get back to these dishes.

Not long after I left the table, my father brought his dish to the sink. Followed by Kita, Isaac then mother. When everyone left, I was the only one in the kitchen. It was quiet and I felt lonely. In times like this, Kita would be waiting for me, so that we could have our conversation. Right now, the only thing to comfort me was the low murmur of the television in the next room.

My father had recently started smoking again, after a month of quitting. We all knew he wouldn't keep his promise for long, so when the smell of cigarettes filled the house, no one was surprised. Around the second week of him trying to quit, I noticed he was taking his lighter to work, so I knew that he had started again. I of course know that battling addiction would never be easy, but judging by the type of man he is, he just doesn't accept help or pity from anyone. He was brought up believing that a man is a person who solves things on their own and should be strong for the strength of the family. Many parents are not open-minded and it's this mentality that ends up destroying many families. With times changing, people have to change as well.

Although I did not fulfil any duties today, I was satisfied with the outcome of the day and was preparing myself for another day of nothingness. I had been tired all day, so best believe that when I went to bed, I fell asleep really easily.

I was a little bit sad, nothing new.

Chapter
V

"Happiness lies in virtuous activity, and perfect happiness lies
in the best activity, which is contemplative."

Aristotle

I woke up to my sister fumbling around my room. She pulled apart the curtains and the morning sun hit my face. She pulled the sheets off my body with so much force, I couldn't resist but fight back.

"Kato, get up." She was standing directly above me with her hands on her waist. The sun shone brightly behind her and for a brief moment- she looked like an angle.

"Kita, what are you doing?" I struggled to get up and get a good look at her face.

"We're going out. Quickly put on something more comfortable and moveable, then some sneakers and meet me in the driveway. Hurry up!" She rushed off.

I was tired and confused. Everything seemed off. I tried my best to get ready as fast as I could. Kita sounded in a rush and stressed, so naturally, I thought something bad had happened. Maybe Isaac has had a panic attack or dad has had a tire puncture.

I ran out of my room as fast as I could and stumbled onto the driveway. This was the fastest I have ever gotten ready. When I got outside, I was tired with my head down and my hands on my knees, trying to catch my breath. Kita was waiting for me to finish while examining her watch.

"What's going on?" I asked as soon as I caught my breath.

I looked around the driveway and nothing bad seemed to have happened. It just looked normal.

"Come on, follow me Wesley is waiting." She answered while running off into the street.

I reluctantly followed her fast as I could, as she ran and ran and ran. I was not fit at all. I stopped swimming classes when I was nine years old because of a near-death experience. Ever since then, I found it hard to exercise. I wondered how I have maintained a small body. I had no figure or muscles or anything extra.

Corey on the other hand was invested in soccer so he was well built for someone our age. My thought of this just added sense to Kita's point of drug usage by kidnappers, or whoever took him.

Kita jogged smoothly. She had no problems with her stamina. I admired her. She had all the good qualities a person could want. Yet, I'd never seen her bring back home or even mention a boyfriend or even a 'boyfriend'. Friends of opposite gender seemed foreign to her, so I wonder what really goes on behind the scenes of her intellectual brain.

We jogged ... or Kita jogged while I ran, all the way to Wesley's home. We stopped outside his home. I was exhausted from what had transpired. I'm sure it was my first time in forever, running for that long that consistently. I sat on the grass panting and trying to get my breath. I was sweaty and my chest hurt. This was not fun at all. My pains had distracted me from asking any questions about why we were here. I couldn't even speak. Before I could rest my body, I heard a voice,

"Stand up Mr Lazy. It's not good for your health if you cool your body down without a proper warm down. And trust me, we are nowhere near finished." Kita said firmly.

At this boss-lady's point, Wesley stepped out of his house. I sprung off the grass and fixed my hair and clothing. Wesley looked good with his long-sleeve polyester black shirt and his tights shorts. He had a sports watch on and his relatively long hair held back by a bright neon pink hair ban.

"Kita, Kato it's good to see you guys." He said as he ran down the steps and onto the grass with us.

I noticed he had called her name before calling mine, even though alphabetically my name came first. Added to that, he knew her through me. Thirdly, we are the same age and classmates. I knew I was overthinking this, but I felt like they were both pushing me away. *Why did they both know about this, I was only told a few minutes ago...*

"All right boys. Given the situation, I want us to visit Middleburg East." Kita said looking, at us one after the other.

She paused, waiting for our reactions.

"Yeah. Yeah! Alright. I'm totally cool with that." Wesley said without hesitation.

This is the same Wesley who was once hesitant to speak to people we didn't even know.

"Kita, are you sure this is safe? How would we enter without being caught? Surely she's home at this time." I expressed my doubt about this move.

Of course, I was unsure whether or not to go. I value my well-being and this wasn't safe.

"I want to start a neighborhood weekly run, every Tuesday, Thursday and Sunday. And I am being for real. We are going to go door to door and register each home with a bargain and advertise my shortish business. This is mainly for community service hours, but I also think many people in the neighbourhood need the exercise." Kita explained with no show of emotions.

"Don't worry Kato. Have faith in your sister ... After all she has never failed us." Wesley said in a tone as if speaking down on me.

"...Yet." I added with a pinch of aggressiveness.

"Oh! I forgot to mention. You guys can't say no because you're technically indebted to me. So, what are we waiting for? We're saving Middleburg East for last." Kita continued to act like we are a gang, and she is the leader.

"Cool. C'mon Kato." Wesley said as he followed Kita.

At these words, we jogged to the end of the street to start with our proposal. We were to meet on 5th avenue and split into each street. We each have to recruit a group. Being the slowest, I'm taking the slowest group with the shortest distance of 3 km. Wesley is taking the 5 km group and Kita is taking the 7 km group.

I felt useless in their whole venture. It's like they have formed their own group... against me. I don't blame both of them. If it wasn't for me, they wouldn't know each other. So any feelings I have, are brought on by my actions.

With those ugly thoughts aside, we visited each home door by door. Some let us in, but others politely declined. To those who accepted, we had them sign a register with their home address, telephone numbers and names. We then told them to wear night sportswear since all the running would be done from 6:00 to 7:30 pm. Some homes were really nice. Those were the houses around Wesley's place, with tall walls and lots of glass, clean and looking fairly expensive.

When we neared our home, the houses got smaller and shabbier. Most of the people here did decline and some swore at us for just trying. However, Kita was more energetic than ever. I was happy that she was happy, but my happiness for her happiness started to fade when they would walk ahead of me talking and laughing in secret. It hurt me a lot, but I didn't say anything because deep down, I was mentally preparing myself to meet the mysterious lady that I would have to face one more time. The closer we got to her house the more I started to withdraw. Even though we had been active, the thought of meeting her sent shivers down my spine and made me cold.

Soon enough, the time came when we had to face her. She had the biggest house in the neighbourhood. Unlike anyone else, she had a huge seven-meter-long iron gate which, after all these years, doesn't have a spec of rust on it. She had however had a buzzer installed, so one can ring it and she can answer you from the safety of her home.

Kita was the bravest, but obviously, none of us would, so, she rang the bell and waited. We were patient because we were scared. We didn't bother to ring twice. We were all scared of what she may do if we did. After a few moments of waiting, we heard a crackle then a reply.

"Hello there." The voice said shakenly.

"Good day, ma'am my name is Kita from Meek Girls High. My brother and one friend of ours was wondering if you are interested in taking part in our community service activity." Kita sounded so confident and she didn't even flinch like the rest of us did at the sound of her voice.

" Well, young lady, this is my first time ever being invited to take part in such. What is this activity? May I ask?" Her voice was soft. She spoke slowly and had an odd accent.

"Thank you, ma'am. If you would like to know more, we are happy to come in and share." Kita added.

Silence reeked for a second as only the low hum of breathing could be heard through the tiny speaker.

"Ok darling. But just for a short while." A response hit us all by surprise.

"Thank you." My bossy sister responded.

As soon as we heard the sound of the speaker end, we looked at each other with terror; Kita's terror might have been excitement. Before we knew it, Ms Murry opened her magnificent gate and we walked in. Huddled up together, we kept close to one another. So close that we made sure a part of our bodies were always touching.

Despite the size of the house, it was extremely clean. This includes the outside. There was not a single leaf in sight. I took note of the surroundings and especially the way we entered.

"Guys look," I pointed out, *"It's beautiful."*

There was a big fountain in the middle of her driveway. This fountain was still working and looked extremely well kept. It was adorned with mini-statues of babies, very strange but what was I expecting?

I did not want to make it look suspicious that I indeed came here for the purpose of snooping, so, I made it as subtle as ever. While we were still walking up, we heard a loud clanking noise and then a huge door opened up revealing Ms Murry.

There she was. Standing, watching over us. She was way younger than I anticipated- the only thing that would convince me that she was a day over 30 was her platinum grey hair. No wrinkles, no sad eyes. Standing there in a black velvet dress (probably from the 70s), body tight, revealing the body of someone who cared deeply about their health. Her makeup was light but suited her well. The bright red lipstick matched her striking blue eyes. I shifted behind Kita like a young child seeking refuge behind their parents, I was so close that I could smell her shampoo, it gave me great comfort.

"Hello Kita and friends." She had not forgotten Kita's name.

"Good morning Ms Murry." Kita brought out her hand, indicating that she wanted to shake it.

Ms Murry grabbed it firmly, and they maintained eye contact for a second too long.

"Uh, may we come in?" Kita stuttered.

From the moment we rang the buzzer, this is the first time I caught a glimpse of fear in Kita.

"Sure. Why not? While we're on that, would you like some tea?" Ms Murry turned and began walking into the home.

"Yes please." Kita was about to follow, but first, she elbowed Wesley and me because we were just standing there looking at her.

Creepy?

Maybe. But we were in shock about what just happened. When we entered the home, we noticed that you could see two staircases on the far sides of the walls going up into what was known to us from the map as the second floor. Second floors were generally the housing area and where we were most likely to find Corey.

The floors were wooden and neatly polished. This home looked like Wesley's, but three times bigger and it didn't smell like anything at all. It was really weird how it had no smell at all. The harder I tried to find the smell the harder I found it to breathe. Of course, I didn't mention a word to anyone for the fear of getting scolded or worse.

Finally, after a while of walking and passing many doors, we entered the dining hall which was the centre of the home. It was directly above and under everything. It was not a four-wall room. It was rounder with no corners with three ways to exit; to the kitchen, to the living room and back to the hallways.

We sat down next to each other at this thirty-two-chair dining table (yes I counted).

"Excuse me while I go get your tea." She said, getting up to leave.

"Ma'am, if you need any help, I don't mind going to get it for you." Kita volunteered.

"*Wow, you are such a helpful, respectful young lady! Thank you. All the tea is in the fourth cupboard down seventeen left.*" She semi-instructed.

With that, Kita got up and left us alone with the creature.

When she was gone, Ms Murry moved her gaze from Kita to Wesley and me. Her eyes seemed to be studying us, but her body was displaying no emotion whatsoever.

"*You boys certainly feel interesting. So, while we wait, tell me about your community service project. I am intrigued by your courage. No one has ever asked for my participation in a community event since... Never mind, go on.*" She chuckled. "*Also introduce yourselves. I want to know who you are.*"

I cleared my throat and reassured myself that there is safety in numbers and there was no way she would win.

I thought about it for a moment. I suspected that Corey would have mentioned something about his best friends Kato and Wesley in those letters, so the only thing I could do to preserve my safety was to lie, "*My name is Yanis and Kita is my older sister, this is my best friend Prescott.*"

I had to lie for Wesley as well in fear he might not catch on.

"*My sister is doing her last year before university. So basically, to show qualification you need to get over one hundred hours of community service. She is nearly there but she wants to do something more extreme so that she brings back a sense of community and togetherness because ever since that boy Corey went missing, she has felt that we need to bring the people together."* I made sure that I was loud enough for Kita to hear every word.

"Your sister sure is intelligent and should be a valuable asset to her school. Prescott, would you mind just elaborating on the details?" Ms Murry shifted all of her attention to Wesley.

I gave out a huge sigh of relief, grateful that I didn't mess up.

Now it was up to Kita to carry it on.

"It's a weekly sport run which would be taking place every Tuesday, Thursday and Sunday from 6:00 - 7.30 pm. Yanis will be taking the 3 km run. I will be doing the 5 km run and Kita will be taking the 7 km run. All ages can come and yeah, so basically, that's the whole project." Wesley spoke.

Kita walked in with a tray, on it was hot water, tea bags, sugar cubes and four tea cups. She set them at the far side of the table closer to where Ms Murry was, forcing us to get up and get closer to her. I got up and began the walk to the tea. I thought that I heard Wesley say,

"Yanis wait for me."

His shirt got stuck in between one of the cracks in the chair. I knew it wasn't serious but saying our names out loud would be the only way to get Kita to catch on, in case she missed out.

"What's up Prescott, don't be so childish and get up." I put emphasis on his name just to make sure.

I then walked over to where he was struggling and pretended to help him out. When he was out, we made our way to get some tea. On passing Kita, she and I caught eyes. I gave her a wink to which she responded with a smile.

In preparing my tea, I made sure to not add anything extra. Just a tea bag and water. I was not fond of having plain tea, but I made sure to make the signs clear to Wesley so he does the same.

When we were seated, we continued to elaborate more on the project. After a while, we got her to sign up to attend. Unfortunately, it was discovered that since she was still a beginner, she would be coming with me on the 3 km stretch. Of course, I was both anxious and bothered, but the thought that she had to be brave to try anything out in public put my mind to ease.

"This may be off-topic ma'am, but Prescott here is quite new to the neighbourhood and I was wondering if you could give him the fascinating history of the oldest building in town." Kita said, sitting up on her chair.

"How old is this building?" Asked Wesley.

"How big is the building?" I joined in.

"Alright, alright. I shall feed your young minds, you curious little ones. Note you are the first group of people I am doing this for.

A n d, I have rules. Do not open any doors or enter any room without permission. Do not touch anything and always follow me". She was clear.

"It's an honour, I will make sure they follow the rules." Kita said, trying to sound grateful.

"You could say this is sort of like a tour, but of my house." Ms Murry added, with some effort to be humorous.

We all forced out a laugh.

She got up and was making her way out of the room when she called back, *"Come on now, follow me."*

We all struggled to get out of our seats as fast as we could and rushed out of the room to start our journey with hopes to uncover some secrets of the Middleburg East home.

On the first floor alone, we went into so many rooms I quickly lost count. She explained the function of each of the rooms and how they were used for different purposes back in the day. She even showed us the servant quarters that could house at least twelve servants. All the furniture was old but didn't seem to be breaking or rotting anytime soon. It was like someone cleaned here daily, but I've never seen anyone enter or leave this place. The home looks frozen in time. Again, no smell, no wind, no sound, other than our voices, our footsteps on the furnished floor and the tiny creaks as the doors opened.

"Ms Murry, do you ever get lonely living in such a big house?" I asked.

"Yes, I do Yanis. As you can imagine, if you had all this space for yourself." She responded joyfully.

"Do you often get visitors?" I follow up.

"Well, no, because all my family members are dead or non-existent, although, for the past many years, I've found a way of entertaining myself and keeping myself company." She acted on.

"What ways?" I continued.

"Haha, you sure do ask many questions." She said quickly.

Did she wink? I was not sure. But she never answered me, nor said she never would. After her remark, she continued to explain and tell us about the history of this place.

I saw that Wesley and Kita were getting uncomfortable with my interrogative questions, so I decided I would resist asking the other questions that were pounding in my head.

We finally made our way up to the second floor. It had a hallway with many doors. Assumingly the bedroom area. We went through each one as she explained which family members would sleep where and why. I dare not mention that all of the rooms had their own bathroom.

I began to wonder if she had private names for these rooms. At this time, I fought to suppress eight, who was urging me to change my thinking, ... or to divert from listening to Ms Murry.

We were nearing the end of the hallway and she had skipped the last three rooms, claiming that those were where she spent most of her time and weren't clean enough to be shown.

"Ms Murry, how does this house stay so clean?" Kita asked, looking surprised at how clean it actually was even on this floor. *"It looks like nothing has changed since it was put in place."* She added.

"Do you believe in magic?" Ms Murry asked.

"Uh...no?" Kita said.

"Me too. Anyway, let's get moving." I seemed to have instructed.

At this, her tone changed, *"You guys have to be on your way now. I have things to attend to."*

She turned around, pushed her way through us and started walking back. Her demeanour suddenly changed and she became arrogant and pushy. I was trying to figure out why, while following the rest back down the corridor, and then I heard it.

A soft moan and the rustling of sheets come from the second last bedroom. This was one of the three bedrooms that we have skipped. I really wanted to open the door to see if it was Corey, but I couldn't. I would risk everything we had come here for and compromise the whole plan. I thought of a plan to get us out of here as quickly as possible.

I held my stomach and started limping, *"Kita, Prescott I need help. I have a stomach cramp. Quickly!"* I shouted at them.

They turned to see me in agony and reacted fast by each coming to my side and helping me walk.

"Oh my. Yanis, what has happened? Oh, quickly, now we have to get you home." Ms Murry picked up her pacing and was speed walking, *"Do you need a lift? I can organise a taxi."* She asked in complete panic.

"No, it's fine ma'am. We don't live that far. Yanis has experienced this before, so I know what to do. Thank you for your offer." Kita was sure smart.

And so, they helped me down the stairs and out the front door. Ms Murry didn't travel with us to the gate. She just stood in the same position she was in when we entered and said, *"See you on Tuesday!"*

"Thank you so much Ma'am. See you then!" Kita said back.

"Yes. Bye." Wesley and I said in unison.

We walked out of the gate and they helped me a few metres down to the park. I got away from their grip and stood my ground.

"Thanks for that Kato. She was getting weird." Kita said, grateful that we had left for home.

"Yeah, she was. I felt like she was anxious that we were there, after inviting us in." Wesley added almost spontaneously.

"I heard something coming from one of the rooms, it sounded like something was agitated." I said, hoping the others would agree and wouldn't' question me as they had done before.

"Don't you think that that was what she might have reacted weirdly to?" I added without making eye contact.

I was sort of in shock. If I may dare.

"I heard something similar, but it was like a faint rustling of sheets or paper." Kita confirmed, much to my relief.

"Me too, but I just thought it was one of us." Wesley added as he extended an invitation to us, *"How about we go back to my house and talk about what the hell we just experienced?"*

"Agreed." I added.

We all left the park and began the journey back to Wesley's house.

When we arrived there, it was 12:34 pm.

None of us had eaten/drank anything all day aside from the coloured water in the name of tea at Middleburg East and we were physically and mentally exhausted.

Wesley's parents were home. They immediately announced that they would be having lunch at 1.00 pm and invited us to join. Since we had time on our hands, we relaxed in his back garden ... waiting. I lay down on my back staring at the sky.

"So, we can confirm that we all heard that noise then?" Kita reflected.

"We can." I said, sitting up and questioning, *"What do you guys think about her?"*

I had been dying to ask this question. Actually, hoping that one of them asked.

"For the most part, I thought she was really nice. She seemed lonely but intelligent." Wesley responded.

"But there was something wrong with the house. I couldn't pick up a scent from anything - not even Ms Murry." Kita added.

"Same. I couldn't hear anything too. The clocks on the walls made no sound. The tea cups didn't clack when put down. What was stressful was that no matter how hard I concentrated. I couldn't hear Ms Murry's footsteps. The only things I could hear were our footsteps and the sound from that one bedroom - and of course your voices." Said Wesley.

"I relate to both of you, but did anyone notice the lack of air/wind flow? It was like when we were there, our senses had stopped working." I said.

In trying to be as reliable as the others, I paused to think why, then continued,

"It also felt to me that everything was frozen in time. Even Ms Murry herself. She doesn't even look her expected age. Everything in the home was nearly a century old, but none of it had begun to become frail or fragile."

"I also thought it was strange. How can one keep a place like that so clean with no help?" Kita said in deep thoughts, looking like she was trying to connect the dots. *"I think we are going to hav-"*

"Wesley and guests, please join sir and madam for lunch on the patio." One of Wesley's helpers called out to us.

"Ok. Coming!" Wesley responded.

He got up and fixed himself so he looked sort of neat. Kita and I did the same and left for the patio.

When we entered, we were met by a table of goodness.

"Follow my lead." Wesley whispered as we approached the table.

We took a seat each and on his father's cue, we were led into prayer. After that, we were presented with our lunch plates.

Seafood! We had shrimp, pasta with steamed vegetables, california rolls and rainbow trout.

Nobody spoke a word during the course of lunch. We all just sat and enjoyed the food. The food tasted so good. In fact, it tasted even better because I was hungry. I accidentally ate too fast and ended up being the first person at the table to be finished with their food, so I sat awkwardly waiting for what comes next.

Soon enough, the others had finished.

"Thank you for the meal." Kita said directly to Wesley's parents.

"No worries er- sorry what's your name young lady?" His father answered.

"It's Kita." She responded swiftly. *"Kita."*

"Right, thank you. No worries, Kita. So, tell us more about your community service project. Wesley told us that the project was why you all went out today." His father looked forward to listening.

"Well, uh sir, we went out door to door asking people if they would like to join our running project which will be taking place on a-" Kita went on explaining the concept to them.

"Wesley, you didn't ask your parents to join?" Kita asked, half laughing.

"No, I didn't think they'd be into this kind of thing." Wesley seemed honest.

"Come on now Wesley, you haven't told them about my excellent high school sporting career?" His father answered back jokingly, flexing his muscles and kicking his legs ... under the table of course.

"And mine as a first-team gymnast?" His mother added with just a smile.

"Kita, we would love to join your project, although we are busy most nights. I think that this sort of change is good and needed." Wesley's dad smiled more seriously now.

At this point, Kita walked out. On returning, she handed them the form and they both signed up.

Desert was brought in not long after. We had a single slice of accurately cut-out pieces of cream pie. It was as amazing. Everyone else continued to have a conversation about school, hobbies and even future careers. In all of this, I felt isolated.

Hey eight, how did Wesley find out about Kita's project before me?

She obviously told him behind your back.

But how?

Most likely text or they met up yesterday while you were doing nothing.

Bu-but-.

Face it, Kato, we have to be alone sometimes.

I faked a smile and tried to join in the conversation. My efforts failed and everyone kept on conversing as if I never existed.

"May I be excused to the bathroom?" I asked.

Everyone stopped to look at me as if they had forgotten that I was sitting right there.

"Of course, darling." Wesley's mother replied uncomfortably.

I got up and I walked away.

From a distance, I could hear his father asking Wesley; *"What's his name again?"*

I ran to the nearest bathroom that I could remember (which was quite far). When I got in, I just sat on the toilet seat, not exactly crying, but with a soft but detectable feeling of hatred for all of them sitting out there. With my hand, I clenched my chest near my beating heart, then forced myself to calm down and think rationally. The stupid breathing techniques my school counsellor had taught me didn't work. Instead, I tried meditation. Through, that I could detach myself from this whole situation. I hadn't been meditating lately. Maybe it was what I needed.

I was in the bathroom for a while. I was deep in meditation when I heard a knock on the door that frightened me.

"S-someone is in here." I stuttered with my eyes focusing on the door.

"Kato, are you ok?" It was Kita's voice.

"Yes sis. I am fine. Just had a little tummy ache." I lied.

"Do you need my help?" She asked, attempting to open the door.

When she realised that it was locked, she urged, *"Unlock the door, now."*

I got up to unlock it. She came in and closed the door behind her.

"What do you want?" I asked.

"I just came to check up on you." She calmed down as she set eyes on me.

She really thought that she could say a few nice words and win me over

"Is eight bothering you?"

Ever since we were small, Kita has known about eight. For the most part, she has understood. But now, she was crossing the line.

"No Kita, eight is not bothering me. eight is not the problem I should be running away from."

I pushed her away and got out of the bathroom.

From there, I went to Wesley's bedroom where he was sitting on his bed waiting for me.

"Kato are you ok? I asked Kita to check up on you." He looked up at me.

*"Yes, Wesley I am just **fine**."* I sounded hostile, but my whole point was to make them both uncomfortable.

"Well ok. I guess now we just have to wait for your sister. Or you know what? Let me go find her". Wesley insisted.

"Actually no! She will find her way." He paused.

At this point, I had gotten up, ready to stop him.

"Does she know where your room is?" I was curious about his above statement.

"Yeah, she does. I showed it to her just before she went to get you." He innocently responded.

My blood was boiling again as I snapped, *"And you're right, she'll find her way."*

I sat back down and looked at the floor, waiting for Kita to return.

"Sorry guys. I just had to use the toilet real quick. Anyway, we need modifications on our plan of breaking and entering. The break-in will happen the night of Tuesday the 19th. This is good because it gives Ms Murry a reason to be out with the running club and it's like the least unsuspecting day." She spoke, sort of catching her breath.

"It's also my birthday ... " I opposed.

She knew the 19th was my birthday. They were doing this on purpose. They are making me feel like I'm worthless, while they are bringing down my worth to make me feel like I am worthless.

"Oh my. Kato I'm sorry. I mean, I didn't forget about your birthday or anything. You don't mind. Do you?" Kita patronised me.

She didn't look sorry and she did forget about my birthday.

"No. It's ok." I played along.

It's not ok. I was hurt and what hurt me more is that none of them cared.

"Ok now that it's sorted. On the 19th of June, we meet up at my home to prepare to go lead the Tuesday run. Beforehand, we have all of our equipment set up by the park so that when we leave the run, we just go straight to the park and get our things." She paused, then continued, *"But we need a reason to leave training early, anyone have any ideas?"*

"Oooh, I got one." Said Wesley. *"Kato can have a false injury."*

Looking at me directly, he added, *"Like you did to get us out of the house today. You can do it again, but to get us out of the run!"* He excitingly kept looking at me.

He was only paying attention to me because I could be useful, I thought.

"Why me?" I could not hide my feelings.

"Well, because she already knows you get hurt easily, so, it would come more believable." Wesley did not hesitate.

"I agree with Wesley." My sister threw in.

Of course, you do.

First, they take my birthday. Now they want me to fake an injury.

"Ok. So now that that's sorted, we will have to make our way to the park, grab our gears and from there, you two enter the home and I'll be on the lookout. Remember the SOS signal." Kita continued.

"How will we enter?" I asked because the gate was open with a remote that we don't have.

Attempting to climb that gate would be suicide.

"Holy, right. We haven't really thought that through. Obviously, the gate is a huge no-go. If I remember properly, at the back of the property where it shares walls with the old milk factory, there is a door in there leading into the barn, which in the olden days was used for milk and fresh eggs delivery. So, since it hasn't been occupied for a while, I think that the factory ground is the best place to gain access to the property. From there, it will lead you to the basement trap door that we talked about. And same drill from the bottom up." Kita clarified.

"Ok, cool," I said. *"Is that it? Can I go home now?"* I sort liberation.

I just wanted to leave. To get away from these two.

"Well yeah. Everything is good to go. We will meet up again during the weekend." Wesley said.

"Friday at mine, Saturday and Sunday at yours?" He added.

"Deal." Kita said and they shook hands.

"Ok. Well, see you at school Wesley." I said as I walked out of his room.

I did not wait for them to follow because right now, that was not in my interest. I picked my walking pace and soon enough, I heard them following after me down the stairs and through the hallways. On my way out, I made sure to say thank you to the helper who served us lunch. Then I walked out.

I could hear them talking to one another in a low whisper about who knows what. I was angry. *I am angry.* I broke into a sprint. I have had enough of their voice and insensitivity. As far as I could tell, I meant nothing to them. So, they meant nothing to me also. I ran like my life depended on it. I didn't have this strength in me earlier today. This time, what was running through me was pride. Kita and Wesley noticed that I had taken off. Yet, none of them had done anything.

I hate them eight...

Well hatred without expression is harmful.

Expression?

Yes, you have to let them know how you feel.

But wouldn't that ruin everything?

Yes and no, if they find you and your feelings valid, then they would listen to you and try to find a solution.

How do you think I should do it?

Through words.

I'll wait until the plan is over. I don't want to mess things up.

I agree, wait until it's over.

But until then, relax this new behaviour of yours.

Ok.

eight was right. They need to know how I feel.

When I got home, the first thing I did was shower. Then homework. Then I laid on my bed drawing how I felt. Kita came home about 30 minutes after me. She didn't check up on me or even speak to me for the rest of the day. Nothing could've hurt more than the only support system I had turning their back against me. Now, I was all alone like I was once upon a time. It didn't feel great.

I went on with the rest of my day without a word to anyone.

Chapter
VI

"Happiness lies in virtuous activity, and perfect happiness lies in the best activity, which is contemplative."

Aristotle

Monday morning.

I hated the thought of going to school. Having to spend uncomfortable moments with Wesley for six plus hours a day was too much. It was the worst thing that could happen at the moment. I had to find a way to still attend school but dodge any type of conversation. Then it hit me; a master of manipulation plan.

The target of this plan is my teachers. All I have to do is avoid break for the next five days and get to change seats. In order to do so, I needed to give the teachers some type of excuse. It was hazy, but all the details were there.

When I got to school, I didn't stop to say "*Hi*" to Wesley. I went to every teacher that I would be seeing today and I pleaded with them to move my seating space so that I would not be seated next to Wesley. Lastly, with a satisfying report, I went to my art teacher and negotiated to come in at break for the whole week to finish up my art project, instead of taking it on through the

mid-term. Thankfully, all teachers had agreed to my plea, if they hadn't, I might've had to use my ultimate tool - crying.

Some were worried because I was vague about my reason for not wanting to be with Wesley. They all knew that he was literally my only friend.

After speaking to my art teacher, I made it down in time for the first lesson.

Before I could sit down, the voice of the saviour I was waiting for echoed through the class, *"Excuse me Kato, but you will no longer be seated next to Wesley due to your disruption in my lesson."*

"But sir I-" I pretended to talk.

"No excuses, please find a new spot." He insisted.

So, I did. It went smoothly and to even it out, I turned around and mouthed the words S-O-R-R-Y.

That was the routine in all my classes. Some would move me. The others would move Wesley. Some moved another student to replace or exchange with one of us.

After each lesson, I met Wesley in the hallways and we talked about the class and how crazy it was that every teacher was constantly moving us. At break time, I told him that I had break detention for low marks in Phys Ed, so I'd meet him in the next lesson. I then slipped away into the art classroom where I would sit down with my lunch and carry on with my project.

With the first day finished, I was happy with the results. School wasn't so bad after all. Not when I could work around all my problems. When the end of school came, I met Wesley outside the classroom and we talked about how we haven't been able to talk all day.

"Yeah, all the teachers just kept on moving us. Anyway, how's your sister?" He asked.

Yes, Wesley asked that. He has started putting her first. It wasn't 'how are you?' It was 'how is your sister?' I had to leave.

"Oh, damn. I just remembered that I have to pick up Isaac from school on my way home. Catch you later Wes." I responded and I sprinted, away from him and his stupidity.

It's unfair.

Promise me you won't cry?

I promise eight.

When I reached home, I dropped off my stuff, completed my routine and stayed in my room until dinner time. At dinner the table was silent. Just how I wanted it. After dinner, my father sat to watch evening news while smoking his cigarettes and my mother helped my brother do his homework. Luckily, it wasn't my week to attend to the dishes, so I went to my room to try to focus on my school work. I couldn't do my work. It was like I had a mental block. I just sat there staring at my page as my eyes started to tear up. Then out of the blue; without a knock or warning, Kita opened my door and poked just her head in, *"How's Wesley?"*

I jumped up from my seat clearly startled, *"Wesley? I don't know who Wesley is."*

I shut the door in her face.

I don't care if I was being mean, because they all deserve this side of me. I didn't know what was going on between them, but I did not like it at all ...

Tuesday morning and *seven days until my birthday.*

Today was also going to be the first-night run. I was not excited for it at all. All I needed to do was get through this day of school and I would be just fine. I didn't feel like eating today, so I skipped my meals and just got ready. I didn't care about what I looked like or smelt like anymore. I had realised that if no one cares then why should I?

When I got to school, I visited the teachers whom I had not filled in yesterday on what I needed done. Like yesterday, all of them agreed to help me out. Although the adrenaline rush wasn't the same as it had been yesterday, I was equally grateful. I was able to get through this day and I was happy that it had gone according to plan. Even though I knew that it would never happen. I wanted Kita's whole project to fail. I wanted people not to show up. I wanted it to rain so I could go home and stay away. I knew it would never happen because I wasn't a lucky child. God did not favour me. Not much of my wishes do come true.

I hate both of them. I hate Kita and Wesley.

I hope they die.

When I got home, I didn't bother to shower. I went and completed some homework while waiting for the running deadline. *I wonder if Ms Murry would be there.* My feelings towards her presence were somewhat numb. Also, I had a slight grip of fear.

At 5:30 pm, I changed into my sportswear and waited in the living room for Kita to get ready so we can leave together. I had been waiting for a while when I decided to go check up on her. My fear re-surfaced when I opened the door and she was not there. I decided to go to my mother. She may have the answer.

"Mom, where is Kita?" I was desperate and needed this answer.

"She left for the project already. Why?" Mother answered me.

"No reason, thanks." I held my breath. My blood didn't boil. It had just gotten ice-cold.

I only had a few minutes to spare before 6 o'clock, so, I gathered some strength in me and ran to 5th avenue. I had nothing left to think of this situation. I have said everything. Added to this, I couldn't possibly get hurt more. My body was weak from the lack of exercise, but when indulged in a certain goal, my body can be pushed to new heights. Right now, my goal was to get there in time.

When I arrived, I could see a crowd of people doing what looked like a warm-up. In the front of them leading the groups were Kita and Wesley. They came here together without me. *Without me!* I had no choice but to go and lead with them.

"Right guys, here we have our third and last instructor who will be going by the name Yanis. He is a bit late today, but we are glad he is here." That was Kita addressing the many people about me.

I recognised a few faces from school and from the door-to-door advertising. So, why was she using the fake name from the Middleburg East visit?

I was searching the faces for Ms Murry, but she was nowhere to be seen.

I just played along with Kita's introduction because there had to be some good reasoning. We had finished the group warm-up. We split into the groups of people we would be taking.

"Hi, I'm Yanis. Welcome and thank you for attending. I will be acting as your instructor taking you all through the 3 km run. As we begin please follow me and stay behind me at all times. If you need help, speak to me and I will attend to you. If you get tired, I will slow the pacing for everyone. Remember that we run as a team, stay together." I was ready.

I made sure to start everyone off at a slow pace and increased it slowly as we went on. For the first few minutes, everything ran smoothly with no disruptions. Everyone was keeping up and no one had sustained injuries.

"Hi, Yanis." The voice was familiar.

Too familiar.

I turned around to see who it was. It was her.

She increased her pace. So now, we were running together at the same pacing. She looked different. I couldn't identify her face earlier because she was wearing these dark sunglasses; even though it was getting dark. She wore a two-piece black tracksuit which nicely gave everyone the correct outline of her figure. Everything she was wearing looked fresh and brand new.

"Hi Ms Murry. You look so different with those glasses, I didn't notice you earlier." I said

"Well dear, that's the point..." She said

"I'm glad you were able to make it." I responded.

Not looking directly at her, but focusing ahead.

"Me too. I think that this is lovely. Having such a heart-warming community event which is also well attended. Well done to you and your friends. I cannot express enough of my gratitude for the invite I received." She sounded truly grateful.

Poor lady must feel so alone.

"Thank you, ma'am. I think that a good way of expressing that gratitude is showing up for every run and maybe even encouraging others to do so. You know, the more the people the better the impact." I could still not look at her.

"You're a smart child Yanis. So, tell me what origin is your name? It sounds odd." She inquired.

"Uh-uh, well ma'am, my parents didn't necessarily choose my name. Their relatives did. So, to be honest, I have no idea." I lied.

I could not let her know anything about my personal life. Just the slightest mistake could have her suspicious.

"I like your outfit ma'am. Very modern." I diverted. A normal conversation would certainly help.

"Thank you. I went shopping yesterday to find the perfect outfit for this occasion. It's not often things like these happen."

"You're right and I think that this is a step for more community events."

I quite like her. She didn't seem hostile or weird. She seemed to like me too.

I smiled!

You don't like her Kato, you're just lonely.

No eight. I think I know my own emotions. I admit that I am lonely, but there is just something about her… I don't know what.

Do you like her then?

Yes. I like her.

For the duration of the run, we talked about our favourite colours, our favourite fashion styles and the types of outfits we like. For an old lady, she had a lot on her mind about what she wanted. She was quite educated in the modern world and about how we ... the young live.

Unlike most adults, including my parents, who didn't understand what living young was like, Ms Murry seemed to have a lot of her youth bottled up inside of her. She was like any other teenager, except that, she was five times older than the oldest teen on earth.

Soon, our 3 km run had come to an end.

It was my job to finish off the evening, "*Before you all leave, we will have to do a quick group warm-down to prevent our muscles from hurting. After we do so, you are free to grab some water, have a quick chat or go home.*"

I led the warm-down.

"*Thank you once again for coming, don't forget we're still on for Thursday.*"

Many people gathered up to talk and some left to go home. I was alone waiting for Wesley and Kita to return. I sat down on the bench and stared at the grass.

"*Boo!*" Someone said as they touched my shoulders.

"*Damn!*" I turned around to see Ms Murry.

I didn't hear her footsteps. I didn't hear her coming.

"*Do you want me to keep you company while you wait for your other friends to return?*" She sounded concerned.

"*Oh! Jeez ma'am, you scared the hell out of me ...*" I responded, trying to be playful.

"Oh! It was just a bit of fun. Also please call me Bertha." She convinced me.

"Ok Bertha. I would love it if you could keep me company. It wouldn't be safe if I were on my own." I confirmed my fear verbally. It was true. It was quite dark and I needed someone by my side.

"Bertha is an amazing name." I decided to talk on.

"Thank you Yanis. So, tell me what you normally do in your spare time?" She asked while sitting down.

I told her about my art, my writings, my semi-manga obsession and my lack of interest in school. She was listening to me. From what it seemed; she was not just hearing what I was saying. She was involved. This reminded me of when Kita used to do the same.

"To be honest, in my young days, I was a lot like you. I didn't like school, but I did take pride in my dancing and writings. I still remember my first ballet lesson, oh how I miss those days.

I had big dreams to be either a professional writer or dancer someday. Unfortunately, all that vanished when my father married me off to the richest man in town, Earl Murry. Since the marriage was against my will, I did not like him one bit. I found it hard to be affectionate and it soon turned abusive. Our relationship was complicated. Being in the army sure didn't help." She tried to laugh it off but I could tell it was painful.

Ms Murry is opening up and letting me in, irrespective of my age.

"How did you feel when he passed on?" I had to match up.

She responded fast, *"I did not pay much attention to that thought because he had left behind a little baby boy for me to take care of. Sure I was sad, feeling his presence slowly disappear over the years left me empty. So, I spent most of my time with my boy. I would have to say that my little boy was the true love of my life."*

"Excuse me, but did you say 'was'?" I was keen on what their relationship held.

"Yes. I did. Sadly, he passed away too at the age of thirteen, can you believe it? A month before his birthday he DIES. Leaving me all alone.

I celebrated his death anniversary last month. Oh! How the Murry family blames me for killing them both. But I would never have hurt my little boy." She seemed disappointed but also hurt as she continued, *"Ever since my boy died, I haven't felt too well, nor have I felt the need to make social interactions. My family wants nothing to do with me. Sometimes, I see boys like you who remind me of him and I...I- Only sometimes, only at specific times."* She looked out of touch like she had forgotten that I was seated right next to her.

"What do you mea-." I could not hold back.

"You remind me of him." She cut me off.

"What was his name?" I asked.

"Klyde. His birthday is on the 21st." She opened up further.

I noticed at this point that her eyes were fixed on the ground.

"Woah. Guess what? My birthday is on the 19th!" I was excited, but I spoke with the intention to distract her from focusing on the ground. I needed that she looked at me, or at least wonder, so I can do a mind-reading exercise.

"Really? Oh, wow. Yanis, that's amazing. We should celebrate." She supported me.

"Yes, I thin-" I extended some kindness.

"Yanis! Hi." Wesley said as he ran over.

He had just finished up with his group and was waiting for Kita. I guess. Ms Murry and I were so deep into conversation that we didn't even hear the chatter the new group had brought on. Or at least, I did not hear.

"Hey Prescott, how did it go?" I asked.

"Who is this with you?" He completely ignored my question.

"It's Ms Murry. Remember her?" I responded calmly.

"Of course, I do. Hi ma'am. It was a pleasure having you here today with us. How did you like it?" Wesley addressed Ms Murry without looking at me.

Ms Murry's face changed. Her expression indicated to me that she didn't like Wesley's presence at all.

"Today's run was great. Having Yanis by my side made it all more enjoyable." She turned and smiled at me.

I smiled back.

"Good. Good. Do you mind if I sat here with you? Just until Kita gets back and we can all leave?" Wesley spoke to me this time.

"Well, I was just about to get going. I have things to attend to back at home. You all have a good night, boys. And Yanis, let's continue this another time." Ms Murry got up, grabbed the little bag she had with her and walked down the street.

I kept my eyes on her the whole way as she walked so majestic in her footsteps. She walked off into the distance and disappeared. I sound crazy, but it happened. She wasn't there anymore or maybe my eyesight was just bad. I couldn't see her.

"Sooo, what did you guys talk about?" Wesley broke the silence as he sat down in the same spot Ms Murry once did.

"It was nothing really. She was just telling me about her fashion style and her favourite shops. We talked about art for a while and the different types. You know it was pretty normal." I told.

He didn't deserve to know about Klyde or anything about her personal past. Ms Murry told me this information because she trusted me and I am sure as hell did not trust Wesley.

"Awfully basic Kato. I expected you to find out more about her. But I guess you still have time, right? Two more running sessions to gather up as much as possible. Anyway, my running time was great-"

So, he talked and talked and talked.

I didn't bother to listen to him brag about how amazing it was. Wesley clearly wasn't the same person I once thought I was in love with. He was becoming more self-centred as the days went by. I feared that if I did not change, I would be left behind. It actually looks like one cannot force change upon oneself but I should try, for the sake of my sanity.

"That sounds great Wesley." I said, trying to sound enthusiastic.

"You've been acting differently lately. More at a distance." He tried to receive some type of conversational intimacy.

"Nope, I think that you have been the one acting differently. I feel just fine." I fought back in calmness.

"Well, no, because I have been feeling an awful lot of hostility within our relationship." He added.

"I doubt it. But it seems that you and Kita have gotten closer while I am getting more 'hostile'." I tried not to let my feelings of anger get the best of me ... again. I had to keep my

statements vague so that I didn't mess up our plan before it had taken place.

"We aren't getting closer. We just found a common interest and find it entertaining to talk about." He justified.

"That's so cool Wesley." I said sarcastically.

He was trying to tell me that we had nothing in common, which was correct. I enjoyed his company but we didn't really connect. Even our art were two totally different worlds. I guess you could say he leaned more onto the academic side, while I was more on the art side.

"Thanks. I hope you understand though. I don't want her to come in between our relationship." He explained further.

I didn't understand. If you didn't want her to impact our relationship, then why did you follow through?

He just doesn't think what he is doing is wrong. That is the overall problem.

"Hey boys. How are things going?" Kita was here.

Again, I didn't hear her group pull up or hear them doing their warm-down.

"We're good. How was your session?" Wesley stole my lines.

Not like I cared anyway. But does he have to ask her just like I did him?

"Mine was great. I'm sure we'll have time to reflect later. We finished later than I had expected, so we have to rush

home. "She grabbed her backpack and started walking down the street.

I followed after her and Wesley joined. The silence was awkward. Nobody said a word. We continued walking in silence. To me it felt like we were afraid to speak, although I was unsure why we would be afraid.

"You know what, since I didn't arrive with y'all I don't want to go back with you either. How about next time inform me on when we go?" I broke out.

I was not going to walk all the way home in that disastrous silence. So, I ran.

The faster I ran, the more liberated I felt. Having silence to myself felt more comforting than having silence with people who do not want to talk to me.

By the end of this all, I'm sure you'll be physically healthier than your mental state.

Not very funny eight. But I agree. I've been running a lot lately. It's not a good or bad thing. I like it sometimes, it makes life more dramatic.

When I arrived home, dinner had been eaten and everyone was doing what they normally do; my dad watching television. My mother and brother together talking or playing or whatever.

I went in, relaxed and took a shower. I then heated up my own dinner and sat alone at the dinner table. Halfway into my meal, Kita came home.

I wonder what took her so long.

I was not going to speak to her until I had received an apology. So, I went the rest of that evening without speaking to her.

When I went to bed, my body hurt. My head hurt and I felt like I had no control over what I was able to feel anymore.

I fell asleep and I felt at peace.

Wednesday morning, another day of school.

This day was like Monday or more like Tuesday (without the run). My teachers had agreed with everything and I avoided Wesley successfully.

I met someone else though. Her name was Anais. She was in my grade but in another class. She had also wanted to get in time on her art project before it was due. At first, we had only shared a greeting. But after a while, that greeting turned into conversations about school then about art.

We spoke about our pieces and what it meant to us in relation to the final project. Anais was a cool girl. She and I had some things in common. Added to that, she didn't seem to get irritated, annoyed or bored at any point in our conversation. She was one of the few people I spoke to at school that day, other than the teachers and students I had been forced to interact with. I must say that thanks to Anais, Wednesday has been the best day of the week so far.

When I got home, I followed my normal routine. At the end of it all, I lay in bed and thought about Anais.

Don't get your hopes up Kato, she might hurt us.

Shut up eight, I'm not thinking about it like that. Plus I won't get attached.

Do you really think you will be able to stay true to those words? To me, it seems that you are already getting attached. You can't get head over heels for someone you met a few hours ago and who may not even be thinking about you!

I'M NOT "HEAD OVER HEELS". I'm just feeling the emotions I have to feel. I can't keep suppressing my emotions you know?

Go to bed, you are overwhelmed.

Psht, you are one to talk. You're the one who should go to bed. Go now!

Good night.

Good night.

Thursday morning.

Four days until my birthday.

The second day of the night run. I woke up more refreshed and excited. I wasn't sure where the energy suddenly came from, but it felt good.

When I got to school, I didn't visit any teachers. I was confident and I had decided after the conversation with eight that I would no longer suppress my emotions. That I should rather face them head on. No running away from them, then turn around and make impulsive decisions. In the lesson where I sat next to Wesley, not a single word was exchanged. He didn't look at me or anything. He just kept his eyes forward. I couldn't read his facial expression. If he felt guilty or upset or too proud to apologise, I could not tell. Whatever he was feeling, he kept it to himself. I did too. He succeeded. Did I succeed?

At break time, I sprinted out of class to get to the art room a little bit earlier than Anais. When I got there, the room was empty just as I thought it would be.

I sat in my usual spot, brought out all my things and started focusing. A few minutes later, Anais showed up.

"Hey Anais. How are you today?" I welcomed her.

"Hey Kato. I'm good. I didn't get that much sleep last night though." She responded.

"Yeah. Me neither. But I woke up today really energised." I took a deep breath in and focused on my words to avoid a stutter.

"Do you mind if I sit next to you?" She enquired.

"No not at all. Make yourself comfortable." I responded and shifted to make space for her.

She sat down next to me. We were so close that the tips of our knees were touching; My right knee touching her left knee.

"So, do you think that you'll be finished before mid-term?" I asked.

"Yes actually. Well, I hope so. I just want to take the mid-term and relax you know? Because lately school has been a total overload. How about you?" She enquired.

"Well, I am doing this partly because I don't want to make uncomfortable contact with a friend of mine, but I guess it could relate to yours. I want to relax or just think things through during mid-term. This hasn't been the best few weeks for me." I used the truth as a means to gain her trust and maybe make a friend. I needed a friend.

"Is it that guy Wesley you always hang around with?" She asked.

"Um yeah. You know him?" I was surprised.

"Well, I always see you two together. You guys seem to be very close, some people in the grade think you're dating each other. If you continue dodging him you'll hear rumours that you guys broke up. What happened?" She had stopped painting and looked at me wanting to know more. She looked genuinely concerned.

"Wait, dating really?? Wow. Well I guess we were dating at one point." I looked at her for a reaction.

"Ugh, I knew it!" Anais looks proud.

"I'm just joking loll, we've never been THAT close but basically after what happened to Corey, I guess we started drifting apart. So basically, now I'm friendless." I said.

I couldn't look at her in the eye. Something about her made me feel uneasy. I gave a faint smile and tried to brush it all off as I said, *"I'll be ok though. I'm sure of it."* I felt like I lied to her. But even if I did, the truth is that Wes and I would not have been going through what we are experiencing now, had our friend been here... or say around.

"Are you sure Kato? Not having friends is hard, trust me I've been there. Plus, you have me as a friend, right?"

I was shocked that she thought of me in this way. *I have a friend?*

"My friend? Oh, wow um yeah sure... thank you Anais. It means a lot." I sounded corny, or cringy. But the words didn't flow as I expected them to.

"Why're you thanking me? A friendship is mutual silly! I myself don't have many friends. So, having you is quite valuable." She ascertained me.

At that moment, I saw some vulnerability in her, indicating that we felt the same way, but expressed our feelings in different ways.

"I like how strange our names sound. It's not like we see a Kato and an Anais every day." I laughed.

She laughed with me.

We both returned to our artwork in silence. This silence wasn't the awkward kind I felt with Kita and Wesley last night. Anais and I weren't afraid to speak to one another. We had just become so used to the silence that it didn't bother us anymore.

Anais was certainly special and despite what eight had advised, I may have become attached to how she made me feel. She made me feel safe and certain. She made me feel like me.

"My sister runs a night run club that is being held tonight. I was thinking, maybe you can come? I mean that is if you aren't busy." I don't know why I asked her, but this felt right.

"I think I'll have to check up with my gran before anything else. Where do you meet up?" She asked.

"W-we meet on 5th avenue at 6 pm." I hesitated a little.

"Aww right at dinner time." She complained.

"I know right? Dinner isn't even my favourite meal of the day. But I still dread missing it." I replied.

"Same. But let's be honest, breakfast is by far the best meal time ever." Her excitement level went up.

"I agreeeeeee." We both burst out laughing.

I didn't feel insecure about my teeth or was not self-conscious about how I looked. I felt just fine.

"You're funny. I'll see if I can make it tonight. Can I get your cell number?" She said, struggling to hold back her laughter.

"Sure-"

I gave her my phone number and just then, break was over.

She got her stuff and just as she left, she looked back at me as I was packing up my stuff and said, *"Hurry up Kato or you'll be late."*

And she disappeared.

I didn't care about whether I would be late or not. Hmm, of course, I wouldn't tell her that. I didn't want to give her the wrong impression or make myself look bad. I wanted to keep her as a friend for as long as I could. Even if that meant twisting the truth. No! not twisting the truth. Twisting how I express the truth.

The rest of my day was as normal as it would get. Wesley and I didn't speak and for once, I was actually focusing on my subjects and school. As the saying goes; *You win some, you lose some.*

It sounds funny, but maybe this is my academic awakening. Although it's a little bit late in the school calendar, I'm sure I can still bring up my marks and make my parents proud.

At the end of the day, I went home all by myself on this calm afternoon. Everything was brighter and more vivid. I was happy today. I haven't been in a long time. I wasn't thinking about Wesley or Kita. They are problems of the past.

When I got home, I changed into the same sportswear I had worn on Tuesday. Of course, it was washed. I'm not a dirty person. I did any homework or schoolwork that was outstanding. When that was finished, I waited for two things; Anais to text and the time for me to go.

It's been about 3 hours since she promised to text me, or since I've given her my number. I know these things take time, but I couldn't help feeling as if she was ignoring me. I had only ever had two conversations with her. At this point, I couldn't really judge her character. I just had to hope that she would communicate with me in one way or another. If not, my only other hope was to see her at school ... tomorrow.

With those thoughts aside, and since I was bored, I waited for time to pass by sitting in front of the television watching some cartoons. I don't enjoy watching television. It's boring and usually has nothing that interests me. The age limit seemed to be a problem and even just the show selection made me disgusted. Here I was today, watching the same shows I displayed dislike for.

I checked the time 5:08pm. I still had time. But I was bored. I decided that I would arrive earlier than everyone else. I had nothing better to do, so why not walk?

I put my things together. It wasn't much though. Just a water bottle and a neon green vest so that when it was time we run, people driving would be able to identify me in the dark. I never usually brought my phone around but just in case Anais texts me, then I should have it handy.

I left the house and began the walk. The vivid things I had seen on my way home seemed to become dull. I wasn't as happy as before. eight was right. I had gotten my hopes up for nothing.

I warned you, you're stupid.

You did warn me. I'm sorry.

You say you're sorry, but you don't know how to change, maybe I should stop wasting my time.

No eight, we both know that we need each other... I don't know, but, until you can find me the magic I need to be able to contain my emotions. I will continue to get hurt. It really sucks.

You're pathetic.

Great so now even my inner self hates me. Maybe eight is right. I am pathetic and I keep on getting hurt over and over. Yet, I fall for it every time.

I think I know, but deep down, I have no self-discipline. I can't even focus on school. My dad has always explained to me how my art won't be able to pay for the good life I want to live and how I should study astrophysics when I go to university. I hate science, but I'm at the point where I will do anything to make anyone happy and appreciate me for my effort.

Anything.

I arrived on 5th avenue at 5:21pm.

It was empty. No one was around. I made myself comfortable and sat on the bench that I shared with Ms Murry the night of the last run. The programme only started at 6 pm, so I felt dumb for arriving so early. I had put myself in an uncomfortable situation where I was all alone with nothing and no one to protect me.

I picked up a stick and started playing around with it. I was on high alert on incoming sounds, footsteps and voices, as well as anything I could detect which seemed even a little bit suspicious.

After a while of playing, I heard footsteps and the soft sounds of voices. In curiosity I looked up only to see Kita and Wesley walking my way. They seemed to be in deep conversation with one another and didn't notice me staring at them. They approached me and kept walking closer. When Kita looked up and saw me, I quickly looked down and pretended to be playing with the stick again.

From the corner of my eye, I saw her facial expression change and become dull as she jabbed Wesley gently with her elbow. When Wesley saw me, his expression also changed. At this point, they had both stopped talking and continued to walk in silence toward me.

"Hey, Kato what's up?" Wesley asked.

He was acting strange. All of his efforts seemed motivated for the wrong reasons and the motivations didn't come from him. It came from Kita. I could tell.

"I'm good. How are both of you? How was your chat? How was your walk?" I acted friendly. I guess to show them that I didn't really care about what they did anymore.

"It was all fine. Why did you get here so early?" He asked.

"Mhm. It was just a choice. There isn't anything wrong in making choices, right?" I responded.

To that, he said, *"No nothing at all."*

"And you sister dearest, long time no talk." Kita hadn't said anything, so I thought that it would be good to include her in this brief reunion.

"I could say the same about you." She put her backpack down.

"You guys sure have changed since I introduced you to one another." I was cracking the ice, but not so that it breaks.

"It's only natural that people change. Isn't it?" Kita responded.

"I don't recall saying it wasn't." This is true. I never said it wasn't.

"Ok Kato you win. But we'll speak about this later." She was avoiding what would happen when we spoke, but so was I as well.

To avoid it further, I said, *"There isn't anything to speak about Kita."*

"Whatever." She walked away to sit on the sidewalk.

"Kato may you calm down a little bit?" Wesley said, looking at Kita as she walked away.

"But Wesley, I am calm." I retorted.

He didn't even bother to respond. He just ran after Kita and sat down next to her. Kita put her head on his shoulder. Just then a sharp pain hit my stomach. I wanted someone who can support me like that. Just anyone.

Before I knew it, people started arriving. Some came in groups, others came alone. Once enough people had come and it was 6.05 pm, we started the warm-up. Whilst doing the warm-up, I got distracted by a figure running towards the crowd. It was still far. As such, I couldn't really pinpoint who it was. The figure started getting closer. As soon as it entered the light, I automatically knew who it was. ... Anais.

Suddenly, I had energy. I was happy again. She stood at the back of the crowd and waved. I waved back. A smile crept up on my face.

She came!!

I wanted to scream.

My worries about being alone had disappeared. I felt revived. I caught Wesley looking at me after I had waved at Anais. *You aren't the only one who can make friends.* I thought.

After the warm-up, we gathered in our groups. Although I was over her, I noticed Ms Murry was here as well. I gave her a brief greeting and she replied. It seemed today she was going to join Kita.

"Bertha are you sure you want to go there? 7 km is a big step." I warned her.

To be honest, I didn't really care.

"It's nothing Yanis. I'm sure I'll be fine. You enjoy." She assured me.

Great. This means I get to spend time with Anais.

Ms Murry left. Anais was not standing far from me. When I approached, her she asked; *"Why did that lady call you Yanis?"*

I knew she would be curious, *"Oh. It's just a nickname I have around here. I'd also prefer if you called me Yanis when we entered this space. Let's get going and we'll chat while we run, ok?"*

I turned to my group, *"Ok, guys, let's hit the road!"*

As we ran, Anais soon caught up to me and spoke, *"It's a weird question but why is Wesley here?"*

"My sister invited him to help lead the 5 km." I was brief.

I didn't want to speak about them right now. I wanted to speak about things we both enjoy. But how do I tell her?

"Must suck having to see him out of school when you can't even interact with him in school." She prompted.

"You don't even know half of it but, I guess now I have to deal with it." I felt the need to confirm her statement.

"Sorry I didn't text you earlier, I can't find my phone. I've seriously looked everywhere! But I asked my gran to look while I'm here and she never fails me." She apologised.

Closure! Plus I didn't have to ask for it. Hurrayyy!

"It's nothing, I understand. I hope you find it." I was so relieved.

"Cool." She concluded.

We jogged together in comfortable silence. Our elbows were nearly brushing against each other but would miss by an inch each time. She was so close; I could feel the sway of wind coming off her as we took each step. I could smell her light fragrance. It didn't smell bad for a natural odour.

We kept on running without a word. I never once tried to compete with her and she never tried to compete with me.

"This run is quite long, isn't it?" I said to her as soon as I felt her steps slowing down.

"Yeah, it is a little bit." She was tired, but still maintained the tone of her voice.

"I'm going to slow down the whole group for a bit. Little by little, so they won't notice a thing." I notified her.

Gradually I slowed everyone down until I felt Anais was comfortable with the current pace.

"Is it better?" I asked.

"Yes. Way better. Sorry though. That I'm not as fit." She apologised.

"Anais! I see you have a thing for apologising but seriously there's nothing to worry about. I'm sure you'll do just fine." I saw the need to assure her. She deserved it.

"Thanks Kat- I mean, thanks Yanis. I appreciate your support." She added.

I'm glad she caught her slip up and I'm also glad Ms Murry was nowhere near to hear it.

"Friends support each other, right?" I pricked.

"Right." She said.

Right until the last step, not another word was shared between us. Our elbows touched once or twice. Each time, we looked at each other in the eye for a brief second before turning away.

"How did you find the run?" I asked as soon as we had finished, seeing that the rest of the group was catching their breath before the warm-down.

"It was quite refreshing for a person who hasn't had any form of exercising for months other than walking." She humbled herself.

"I agree. When I started off, I was just like you. I quickly adjusted." I comforted her.

"Cool. My stupid self didn't think to bring a water bottle, so I am dehydrated as well as exhausted. Man." She tried to laugh it off.

"I have some water and I don't mind you having some." I went to my little bag and got it out. I handed it to her, *"It's fresh from the fridge."* I watched as she drank it. I do not know what to feel.

"All right group, time for our warm down!" I shouted.

We gathered around in our small group and quickly finished our warm-down. Afterwards, some left. Some stayed to chat and some waited for the other groups to return.

Anais and I sat down on the bench and sighed with relief that it was over.

"Sorry, but I nearly finished all your water." She apologised.

"It's ok. If I need to, I'll just steal some of my sister's. No biggie." I responded.

"Sure thing. By the way, what relationship do you have with that lady earlier?" She took us back to Ms Murry.

"She is a friend of my mother's, but she and I are close. Not in a weird way or anything like that." I said.

"She reminds me of my gran. I thought it was her for a second. That's why I looked frozen just staring." She explained.

"That's cool. She is pretty relatable for an old lady." I added.

"I can't imagine." She said.

"I think it's boring, sitting and waiting for the rest. Don't you want to go home?" I asked her.

"I'm good to go home if you want. I don't enjoy being out here either." She responded.

"Great. Let's get going." I ordered.

But before I left, I poured the leftover water from my bottle all onto Wesley's bag. I didn't feel guilt or remorse. What was done was done.

"What did you do that for?" Anais asked while we began our walk.

"It's like prank wars. He was the one who declared war yesterday." The truth, but not the truth.

"To me, it seems that they are too close for comfort." She said.

"Who is?" I asked.

"Your sister and Wesley. I just don't like it." She responded.

"Well, believe me when I say I agree with you, and that it makes me so angry that they can both leave me alone." I added.

"Sometimes I feel the same way." She confirmed my feeling.

"Who left you?" I was curious.

"My mother and father." She shocked me.

"What happened between you guys?" I needed to know

"They both died last year, in a car crash." She said emotionally.

They both died. Anais had no parents. My first instinct was to grab her hand. So, I did and I just held it. This was my first time touching her. She did not resist my touch. We walked the next few metres feeling each other.

Then I asked, *"Can I walk you home?"*

"No. It's ok. I got this." She said.

"But it's dangerous for you to be walking out on your own." I tried to convince her.

"Well at a time like this, I don't really walk. I prefer running home." She tried to out-smart me.

But I insisted, *"I'll run with you"*.

"Thanks for the offer, but maybe another time yeah?" She said.

"Ok before you go one last thing?" I pleaded.

"Sure." She said, looking at me.

"Can I get your phone number so that I can ring your cell and maybe that will help you find it." I requested.

"That's a great idea! You're very smart Kato." She boosted my ego.

She gave me her phone number and began walking away. As she turned the corner, I heard her break into a sprint. I turned around and started walking towards my home.

I detoured, I am in the habit of doing that lately, I have no reason to rush.

After a while of walking, I turned to the last street facing my house. When I was about to continue walking, I saw Kita and Wesley.

They were walking down the street hand in hand. They reached the front door. Before getting in, Kita turned back and gave Wesley a kiss.

A kiss.

A kiss.

I froze. I didn't know what to do or think. I hid in a bush until they had both left. I waited a few minutes just to make sure Wesley had been on his way and Kita was busy, then I started walking back to the house.

When I had gotten in, I went straight to my room. I didn't take a shower or go down to the kitchen for leftovers. I sat on my bed unable to move. This situation was the definition of, "*What you don't know won't hurt you*".

I gathered up enough strength to call Anais. I dialled the number and sat waiting. After the sixth ring, I heard her pick up.

"*Hello?*" She said.

"Hey Anais, it's Kato." I struggled to smile.

"Kato hi. Thanks for calling. My gran found the phone under a pile of books!" She was clear.

"It's no problem. I'm glad you found it. Look, I've run into a serious problem." I pleaded.

"Kato what is it?" She sounded concerned.

I could picture her face. I could visualise her lying down in bed waiting for my response.

"I saw Wesley and Kita - my sister kissing." I sounded urgent.

"Holy crap. When?" Is all she asked as I continued, *"When I was walking home, I-I saw them doing it right outside my home."* I paused for her to talk.

I wanted her to say what I did not even know, but she said, *"I want you to stay calm. Don't overthink any of this. Meet me on 5th avenue before school and we'll talk about this, ok? I don't feel like doing this over the phone will help with anything. I just need you not to hurt yourself by thinking things that are not true."*

"Ok. 5th avenue tomorrow. I'll see you there. Have a good night Anais." I said.

"Good night, Kato. Be strong." She warmed up.

I hung up and fell down onto my back in bed. I thought about all she had said, she was the comfort I needed. If I didn't have her right now, I don't think I would be this pleased.

I couldn't wait to see her tomorrow. I couldn't wait to see her black afro hair. Her dark hollow eyes. Her somewhat crooked teeth. Her nose scrunched whenever she laughed. But most importantly, I couldn't wait to hear her voice.

Anais made me happy.

While I was thinking about her, I got a text message from her. It was a long paragraph of her reassuring me about how everything will be great. To be precise, let me share the message below:

Hey Kato,

I know that you are going through a hard time right now because two of the people you trusted more than anyone else in your entire life had now turned against you and betrayed that trust. I know how you feel because on some nights I blame my parents for leaving me all alone. I overcome those feelings by looking at the good things they have brought into my life. I focus on what can make me. I hope that you can do the same. In life, we face these kinds of hardships and they just seem to make us stronger and more independent. I wish I can tell you that you have overcome the easy part of your healing, but that is not this case. You still have a long way to go, and no matter how far down the way you are, I will always be here for support. I hope you stay strong. See you tomorrow.

Written with love: - Anais.

Why do you rely on people to make you happy?

I don't.

But at the time you had no one you seemed sad but now that you have Anais you seem fine.

Nobody said I'm fine.

No one said it, but I can feel it.

eight, humans need other humans to survive. Not that I need Anais, but having her here surely makes me happier to be alive.

You're complicated.

Unfortunately, I know.

Friday morning.

Three days until my birthday.

This morning I would be meeting with Anais. I got ready in something slightly less comfortable than my average outfit.

I made sure I smelled nice and looked a little bit clean. In the bathroom, I decided to leave Kita a little surprise. I took her toothbrush and dipped it into the toilet bowl then put it back in the same spot.

I told my father that I would be walking to school today and there was no need to wait for me. I left the home.

The morning air was still very cold and it hurt the skin on my cheeks a little bit. But I was still happy. I kept on replaying the message I received last night from her in my head and it just seemed to make things better for me.

When I arrived at 5th avenue, I noticed Anais sitting down on the pavement reading a book. She looked so peaceful, but also very unsuspecting.

"Anais! Hi." I said as I waved to her.

She looked up a little bit confused at first, but once she realised it was me, she smiled.

"Kato! Hello." She quickly put her bookmark in and closed up her book.

She then stood up and as I came closer, she leaned in for a hug.

This hug was long and soft. I was comfortable in her arms. Her smell made my heart flutter and the soft beat of her heart matched mine.

"How are you holding up?" She said after she released her grip and we started walking towards the school.

"Well, I've been a lot better than I thought I would be doing, and it's all thanks to you." I said.

"Me? No, you could've done well on your own. All you need is the support." She responded.

"The support they could never give me." I had my eyes focused on the ground as we continued to walk.

"Here, let me hold your hand." She took my hand and continued, *"I think that both of them have made a big*

mistake. Your relationships will never be the same again. You need to know that you will hurt a lot while trying to heal. Although they haven't done anything illegal-" She giggled.

"Yet, Kita turns 18 in December. Then, yeah, it's illegal." I added.

"Thanks for that. But like I was saying. They haven't done anything against the law. I know you are wishing for harsh consequences." She paused to look at me as I revealed my thoughts.

"What do you think I should do?" I asked.

"Nothing for now. I think that you should take your time to decide on what you want for yourself and for them. When you have decided on the action, I think you should then tell them how you feel. Don't stop them from expressing themselves." She said.

"How do I deal with seeing them? They have ultimately been a big part of my life for a long while now." I fought back.

"I think you have to deal with the truth. Face the truth and don't suppress your emotions." She sounded like eight.

To that, I said, *"Ok. I understand. I'm sorry that I'm a total mess right now and that I'm overloading you with emotion."* I apologised.

"Yikes, Kato. No worries. I just wish I had someone like you when I was going through it, ... you know?" She seemed a little refrained.

"Yeah, I know." I would not let her pronounce it.

We walked the rest of the way to school hand in hand. We talked about our dreams for the future and things we really wanted in life. Through this conversation, I found out that Anais was passionate about how humans may evolve in the years to come and wanted to study the brain of adolescents to find out why we think and act as we do.

I on the other hand had nothing big in mind other than what my father wanted. I enjoyed listening to her ramble on about what she wanted because she seemed so happy.

When we arrived at school, we were still early. So, instead of ditching her as soon as we walked in, I took her to the spot I once shared with Wesley. We sat down and continued our conversation. It shifted from what we wanted to do, to predictions about what the future would hold.

At break, we met once again in the art room. We both managed to complete our artwork. While doing so, we made plans to meet up over the mid-term.

"You know my birthday is on Tuesday." I don't know why I said it, but I was curious about her response. No one seemed to care.

"Tuesday is the 19th, right? Kato, we have to do something celebratory. That is if you have nothing else planned." She showed concern.

"Yes, it's the 19th and no, don't worry about it. I have nothing planned. Nobody seems to care." I said light-heartedly.

"I care. I really do. So, what are you thinking we do?" She asked.

"Anything that won't interrupt the night run time." I reminded her.

"Oh yeah, Tuesdays, Thursdays and Sundays." She refreshed.

We had both stopped talking. Anais looked like she was thinking about something. *I wonder what it was.*

"I have an idea! Oh, my, yes. When I was little, my parents used to take me to Sleslen City, which is like a big theme park with a pool and rides and a movie theatre. Basically, everything a person could need for entertainment." She explained.

"Where is it? I've never heard of this place before..." I showed interest.

"It's a 20-minute train ride out of town. In Nejburg." She said.

"Oh. I see. I think we should go, but I think someone older should accompany us." I realised that we are 15-year-olds.

"Who do you have in mind?" She asked.

"No-one actually." I responded.

"You know, let's forget about it. It's too much money away." She carried on, *"I'm conflicted. I want you to have a good*

birthday, but everything just seems too boring." She seemed to conclude.

"It's ok Anais. We don't have to do anything to feel good. We'll be ok." I assured her.

"I promise, I'll think of something and make this a special day for you." She insisted.

"Cool, cool." I rushed.

At the end of the day, we walked together to 5th avenue and departed from there. Anais didn't seem to want me to see her home or whatever. She kept on refusing and refusing. I didn't want to push her away or make her uncomfortable. So, I just left the situation as she built it.

While walking back home, I started thinking about the whole FC plan and all the measures that would be put into place.

Shoot! We were meant to meet up at Wesley's today.

I got out my phone and called him whilst changing my route towards his home, *"Hello Wesley?"*

"Oh. Hi Kato." His voice was low and had no emotion.

"Yeah. Can I come over to yours?" I asked.

"You're late man. Come on. Kita is already here." He responded.

"Of course, she is. See you there, bud." I hung up and picked up my pace.

When I arrived, I just walked and went up to his room.

Kita was sitting on the bed and Wesley was sitting on a chair facing her. On the floor was everything we needed spread out; the face masks, clothes, flashlights and an abnormal-looking screwdriver.

"Hey guys." I said as I walked in.

"Hi."

"Hi." They each responded in turns.

"This is our last meeting before the day, right?" I asked.

"Yes and no. I figured we should cancel the ones this weekend and have one last one on Monday." Wesley suggested.

"Cool with me." I responded.

"Ok guys, let's get to it. Today, I'm just going to teach you how to use the face masks. How to put them onto yourself and onto others. Then, I'm going to teach you how to pick a lock and those are the steps you should know. Thereafter, you'll be fine." Kita said as she reached down and grabbed one of the three face masks.

She held it in her hand and began her display. She taught us how to put it on properly without breaking it, then how to breathe in an appropriate way so water droplets don't form all over.

After she ran it through twice, we each put them on by following her lead. Thereafter, we tried putting them on her. She positioned herself differently and Wesley and I had to work together to get the mask over her face. After doing that a few times until it was perfected, we then put our arms under her armpits and tried carrying her around. After that was finished, we tried carrying her down the stairs and up. That way we could learn how to be in sync with one another if we had to carry Corey.

After that, she was teaching us how to pick a lock using only a screwdriver. Wesley locked his door. Kita gave us a demonstration of how to do it. We each took turns and tried.

"Where did you learn how to pick a lock?" Wesley asked her.

"I took a self-defense class last year." She answered.

We continued to practice and practice. When it was all over, we went through the routes on the map one more time. This time, with a more accurate feel of the house.

It was the same old. Nothing new.

I left as soon as Kita said, *"Ok. So, I guess that's it."*

I personally didn't have time to be sitting around and having small talk – ok, I did have time, but definitely not with them.

When I got home, I felt mixed emotions. I was happy I was going to see Anais tomorrow, but also disappointed about Kita and Wesley.

Their whole situation had me shook.

But in conclusion, I slept well that night.

Chapter
VII

" The human mind is inspired enough when it comes to
inventing horrors; it is when it tries to invent a Heaven that
it shows itself cloddish."

Evelyn Waugh

Monday morning.

Tomorrow is my birthday.

Tomorrow was also going to be the biggest adventure of my life. My plans for today were simple; try and get some school work and meet up with Kita and Wesley for the last meeting. I would have loved to see Anais, but she had said that she had other plans. She also planned on doing some catch-up on school work. It was quite unfortunate that I couldn't see her, but I also wanted some time for myself, like, just to build up some confidence.

I will admit my school work was fairly boring, but I had put in and made some effort into my academic awakening. After a while of focusing, I had finished all the work that had to be completed during this mid-term. I then sat, and thought about how different life would be if Kita and Wesley had decided not to fall prey to their natural hormones. I would probably be chatting happily with Kita about our lives, while doing our work or would have been with Wesley sharing our emotions about what would be going down tomorrow.

Instead, I sat alone at my desk.

Although I knew that I had Anais, no matter how hard she could try, she would never be able to fill that little bit of me that got taken away by them.

It hurts.

Anais did warn me about all these emotions, but nothing could have prepared me for how shitty they would feel. The fact that I had built such a strong relationship with both of them and that I would have to live with them for the rest of my life regardless of whether they were alive or not, was the worst part of the situation.

But I will live. I don't think I will ever forgive them. But I will live.

At around 3:00 pm, Wesley arrived. We grouped up in Kita's room and discussed tomorrow night.

We first went through the logistics one last time and prepared everything that we would need. We put them in a black bag and disguised the bag in a dustbin plastic.

When that was completed, Kita tried a different approach in an effort to make everyone more comfortable.

"So, guys, tell me how you are feeling about this whole thing." She asked.

"I'm petrified. I'm having second thoughts about going in." Wesley answered.

"Jeez. I'm with you on that. I'm quite nervous as well but not as much since I'm just the watchdog. Remember there is no guarantee that everything will run smoothly, but we just have to trust each other." Kita used that word in a sentence, I was surprised.

"Trust each other?" I asked.

Of course, I didn't want to explode and let out all the anger inside of me. At this point, I had slipped up and needed to somehow save the situation.

"Yes. Trust. Is that a problem?" She said in the cockiest way.

I sort of did what I had to do next, *"No not at all. Is there anything you guys want to tell me whilst we are on the topic of trust?"*

They both looked at each other, then back at me.

"No Kato, there isn't anything we want you to know in particular." Wesley answered, while Kita just looked at the floor.

"I know a secret." I said.

"A secret about what?" Kita asked nervously.

"Not about what but about who." Maybe I was taking it too far, but now it was time to play with their emotions.

"A secret? About who?" Wesley asked.

"Unfortunately, you will only be able to find out tomorrow." I said, making a makeshift sad face.

"Oh. Um. Ok." Kita said, sounding confused.

"Are we done here?" I asked.

"Well, yes. You can say so. Remember to come dressed in the all-black clothes we got." Wesley said.

"Ok. Well, if this is over, I'll see y'all tomorrow. Bye, and don't forget to speak in hushed voices. I can hear you through the walls." I got up while talking, and left.

I have to admit that it felt good. All that I had said and done felt right.

No guilt.

No remorse.

Just happiness.

I spent the rest of my afternoon and evening baking. I don't know why I did it. Sometimes, I have those days in which I just bake. I somehow found it relaxing to do so. Following the instructions step-by-step. Putting everything together and mixing it all up, then pouring it into the pan, or scooping it into the holder, or laying it out on a tray, all seem to give the baker control over the dough.

My favourite part wasn't the eating or the tasting, it was the doing. The mixing and pouring.

Today's baking menu was biscuits. I pulled out my mother's baking book and prepared the ingredients.

I mixed, melted, cracked, hit, and measured the ingredients to perfection.

I put the contents into the baking pan, and proceeded to clean up.

While baking, I heard footsteps.

When I turned around, I heard, *"Bye Kato."*

It was Wesley.

What shocked me is that throughout the time I was baking, he was still in the room with her.

"Bye Wesley. Hope you had fun in there." I responded just before he opened the door.

"I don't know what you're talking about Kato, see you tomorrow." He responded and left.

I continued to clean up my space.

After forty minutes, my biscuits had finished baking and I had them set aside to cool on the countertop. I went back to my room with a few biscuits handy. It was still quite early, so it was unusual for me to be tired at this time of day. I sat up in my bed reading and chomping down some biscuits. Before I knew it, I had drifted off into slumber.

Chapter VIII

" The whole is more than the sum of its parts."

Aristotle

Tuesday morning. My birthday!

It is also the day of the biggest adventure of my life thus far. I woke up at 4 o'clock. I couldn't sleep.

Which sane person could? Despite the amazing weekend I had, there was still a huge sense of despair lingering over me. To help soothe my nerves, I replayed the week that was in my head.

I made sure to focus on all the good bits involving Anais. I could not get Saturday off my mind. It was the day we went to the roller rink. It was magical. Although it was Anais's first time, she was really quick to learn. We had fun going around together. We fell a few times and got quite hurt, but we laughed it all off. Afterwards, we went to eat ice cream in the same shop that Kita took Isaac and I to that one day after school. We talked about the experience at the roller rink and how fun it was. Anais told me about all the cool things she used to do in Nejburg with her parents, like sailing, swimming and dirt biking.

I also thought about my Sunday. On Sunday, we did something less extreme. It was a simple picnic with a little twist to it. We each had to contribute something to snack on, but also bring a small clean canvas with paint and paint brushes. The objective wasn't to do a portrait of each other. It was to paint how we felt when we were together. When I was painting, I found it hard to find an image that displays what I truly feel while with her. This was puzzling to me because I did it all the time whenever I would sketch/draw (which is quite often). Why would I not freely express how I feel about a person I love spending time with? I could not get it, but I soon came up with an idea.

My picture was a tiny black circle in the middle of the page, which signified me. This circle was surrounded by many different shades of colour which signified how Anais makes me feel when I am with her.

At this thought, I got out of bed to fetch the picture Anais had painted during the picnic. We decided to exchange pictures so that we could always be reminded of one another. Her picture was more complex than mine. It was two knives frozen in the motion of colliding with one another. These knives were connected to one person who was pulling the strings. Around that person were thought and speech bubbles. Anais didn't explain to me clearly what was the motivation behind this or how it related to our relationship, but I still adored it equally.

I got out my phone and sent her a message;

'I can't wait to see you tonight xx.'

She would surely find it weird that I was texting her at such a time, but I didn't care. Tonight, may be the last night I ever see her. So, why not be spontaneous about it?

I got back underneath the covers of my bed and made another attempt to sleep. But as I did my brain started playing videos of what it may look like once I set into the home with Wesley. It did a virtual run-through of the whole event without leading me to a conclusion. I then thought of what might happen after the whole situation;

Would I become famous?

What would my parents think?

But most importantly, what would Anais think?

These questions bothered me as my brain ran through possible answers.

Hey eight?

Yeah?

If you had to point out one big thing that made me really unlikable, what would it be?

How you ponder on each word and think everything has some type of deeper meaning, when in reality, some things were created just to be.

Oh, that hurt.

It's true.

I know.

Again, eight seemed to have the answer. Sometimes I wonder how much better of a person I would be if eight and I had switched roles. That is if I was my inner self and eight was my outer self. I would be more confident and less worried. I would be able to provide people with the right type of advice and maybe, I wouldn't hurt so easily.

I got out of bed and went to the kitchen, where I made myself a bowl of cereal, then sat in front of the television. To my luck, I switched on a channel that was playing a crime documentary. This documentary was about a serial killer who targeted young girls. Even though I was not a fan of television, this programme was an exception.

It followed mainly the struggles of the police department as they had little to no evidence suggesting that the disappearance of the girls had even taken place. Like Corey's case, the lack of evidence seemed to hold the police at a major setback. I wondered if they had given up on him like they did the boys before him. The policemen in this documentary had frequently said that the investigation tampered with their personal lives and made things difficult for them; which I can imagine would have been extremely hard. I wish that people who go into those types of professions are given a switch, which enables them to change on and off their emotions. I'm sure a creation like this would save many relationships and hopefully make people happy.

The case seemed to drag on for months. As they struggled to find the killer, families got devastated, losing hope with every day dragging on. But to tie it all together, the killer was caught like in most killer documentaries. He had made a spill up in one of his doings. This eventually led up to his capture.

For me, the most interesting part was not learning about his killings. It was learning about the killer's philosophy and why he chose to kill. I could imagine the insane sensation of pleasure when one would kill, but I couldn't do it, or so I thought.

I couldn't foresee my future. At the same time, no one in their right mind vividly thinks of growing up and becoming a killer.

When the programme had ended, the sun was starting to rise and the noise created by the passing of cars became more frequent. I put my bowl down and returned to my room. My head was aching and my eyes were hurting. I lay down, but this time, I found it easier to sleep.

My eyes closed and I dozed off.

I woke up at 12:00 pm. That is mid-day.

I still felt tired, but I knew that it was no time for me to relax. I got up and out of bed. I took a shower, then dressed up in something nice. I checked my phone to see if I had received any messages. Surely there was one from Anais,

'Why don't we meet up before then?'

I wondered what she wanted to do. Of course, I had nothing planned, so I went with it.

'Sure. Meet you at 5th avenue at 2 pm?' I texted back.

While waiting for her response, I left my room and went to see what I could have for breakfast.

Both my parents had left for work and Isaac for school. I was alone in the house with Kita. It felt cool to have this type of freedom. Every kid I'm sure loved being home alone. It gave us a sense of power. I made toast and had it with butter and a cup of tea. I sat down and put on the television. I turned it on to the news channel while I ate in silence.

While eating and watching, I received a text notification, *'Cool beans, I'll see you there.'*

I smiled at her message. Just knowing that I'd see her already made my day.

I called my mom to let her know that I would be going out. Then, I went into my room. While in my room, I tried on a hundred different outfits. I wanted to look nice when I saw her. Don't ask me why. I finally decided on black sweatpants, a black short sleeve turtleneck and over that, a red button-up t-shirt with a floral print. I looked good. I smelt good. I felt good.

I got some money from my allowance and a small bag for safety, then I left the home. It was only 1:28 pm, so I had enough time to make a quick stop. I went to a small shop just to buy something for Anais. I got her a keychain and a water bottle. There was never anything too extreme to show gratitude towards those you admire. With my goods in hand, I set off to 5th avenue.

When I arrived, nobody was around as usual, so I just sat on the pavement and waited. I didn't mind waiting. There was nothing, in particular, that was disturbing me, so I was fine.

"Kato!" Said a female voice coming from down the street. It was Anais. She was holding a huge basket in her hand. She seemed to be struggling to hold it. Tied to the handle of the basket was a helium balloon with the words, *'Happy birthday'* on it. *Oh yeah, it's my birthday*. I had totally forgotten about it. Maybe it was because nobody had said it yet.

"Anais," I said as I stood up and ran up to her.

"Hi Kato." She said out of breath.

It must have been hard carrying this from her home all the way up here.

"Happy birthday. I have managed to prepare a little something to show you that your life needs to be celebrated!" She handed me the basket. *"Although I didn't really think it through, now you have a huge, heavy basket filled with stuff and nowhere to keep it..."* She thought.

"Anais, thank you so much. You're the first person to wish me a happy birthday." I took the basket with gratitude.

"Really? No one at home did?" She was shocked.

"Correct." I assured her.

"Aww. Sorry." She tried to give me a hug, but the basket was sort of in the way.

"I have an idea. I can take this home with me, then we can chill. Is that, ok?" I questioned.

"That's a great idea." She responded.

"But before we go, I got you a little something. It's nothing compared to what you just gave me." I handed her the plastic with the keychain and water bottle.

"It isn't a competition." She said as she took the things. *"Thank you for the gifts. I will surely cherish them."*

As we walked to my house, we talked and reflected on our weekend. We shared many laughs and feelings of slight embarrassment. We planned for the week ahead and thought about more things we could do together. Seeing as my house wasn't so far from 5th avenue, we arrived there in no time. I knew the house wasn't at its cleanest, but I knew it was tolerable. I invited Anais in, and excused myself to go put my gift down. When I had returned, Anais was still sitting on the couch where I had left her. I sat down next to her.

"So, what do you think of the house?" I asked.

"A house is a house. You could have showed me the biggest or smallest home and my reaction would be the same.

Materials don't make a person happy - or me specifically." She responded.

It wasn't the answer I was expecting. Just like Wesley.

"I agree. So, what do you think we should do today?" I inquired.

"Well, I gave it some thought. Since it is your birthday, and a Friday, I think that we should get a takeaway". She smiled.

"Only fast food?" It seemed strange that she put all the effort only to get one meal.

"Yes, you don't like the idea?" She asked.

"I-I-I- no. I like it. It just took me by surprise." I said.

"Oh great, I'll call ordering! Uh, where is your house telephone?" She asked.

"Wait. You want to order it here?" I asked.

"Yeah. Will that be a problem...?" She was surprised.

"No. Never mind, go ahead. The house telephone is in the dining room. I'll go and fetch it."

I didn't know how I felt about this takeaway thing. I wasn't disappointed, but I wasn't happy either. I wonder what I expected her to say. Not much apparently.

"Here it is." I said, handing her the phone. She took it, and dialled the telephone number.

"How about we go to my room?" I proposed.

"Sure." She accepted.

We went into my room. When the number answered, Anais tried to talk to them but the connection seemed to be really poor. As a solution, she went outside to try find a better signal, while I stayed inside. I used this as an opportunity to tidy up my space. I kept everything that would be a disturbance away and made a clear space on the floor where we could sit.

A few minutes later, she came back inside and announced, *"Food will be here shortly."*

We went into my room where she explored all the different types of books I had neatly placed up on my bookshelf. Each time she saw the ones she liked; she would ask for a summary. If she really liked them, she would ask to borrow them. By the time we had finished looking through all of my books, she had identified 4 books that she wanted to borrow. I told her about my favourite book, why I adore it, why I could read it for the rest of my life, why I felt an attachment to the story and to the characters, why I would kill a man to be able to speak to the author about the book, how the book has helped me with my character development.

While speaking about these things with Anais, we soon came to talk about how we think of ourselves and not each other. One thing led to the next, and I opened up about eight and how I think humans have two sides; our inner selves and outer selves. She agreed with me on humans being born with two sides, but she didn't think that we all had a relationship like I did with eight. Of course, I was not going to try to argue with her about her opinion because I've known all my life that eight was weird. I have come to agree that if it wasn't my family telling me this, it was surely society. Most importantly, I've just learnt to deal with it because neither my acceptance of eight, nor eight itself isn't going away any time soon.

The fast food had arrived when we were talking about how animals would have been surviving long before technology was invented to try and make their lives easier. Crazy how a conversation can switch up right? When we first heard the doorbell, my instinct was to go and open the door, but it was quickly dismissed by Anais telling me firmly to get us plates while she dealt with the order. Of course, I agreed, I went into the kitchen and searched for some small side plates that we would be able to use. Once I had found everything, I went to check on Anais at the door. It seemed that she had dealt with everything before I even got there.

I opened the door to my room and when I looked to the spot where we were previously sitting, there was our food. Beside it, a small circular box. I had a feeling that something was up from the way Anais watched me with a mischievous smile as I was coming towards her. When I sat down and put the plates, I noticed that she was still watching me.

"What?" I said with a comfortable laugh, trying not to look her in the eye.

"Who is going to open the box?" She said, still looking at me. "Wait! Don't answer because I have already chosen you to do both duties." She slightly moved the box towards me.

I took the box. I was feeling nervous. As I opened it, I stared at the food. Spelt out in pieces of sliced pepperoni were the words 'Happy Birthday. Love you.' It may not seem like much, but this is truly the most anyone has done for my birthday ever. When I looked up, Anais was still looking at me. She wanted a reaction.

I gave her a reaction. *"Anais, you have no idea how much all of this means to me. Nobody ever has shown me all this love in a matter of hours."*

"It's ok Kato. I truly care for you and I want you to know that. Guess what's next?" She waited a few seconds before handing the small circular item wrapped in black wrapping paper.

I took it and carefully opened it. Halfway through, I noticed that it was a miniature cake. When I had finished unwrapping it, I lay it so that it was in front of both of us. On the cake were three letters 'HBK.' I didn't know what they meant but I'm sure it was something special. When I looked at Anais, she was still looking at me. Her dark eyes stared straight at me. They were filled with hope and happiness.

Except this time, I couldn't express my thoughts in words. I mean what I thought of her.

"Do you know what the letters mean?" She asked.

"No. Not at all." I responded.

"They stand for Happy Birthday Kato. The cake was too small to put the words on, so I had to improvise." She smiled.

"You made this cake?" I appreciated.

"Yes, I did. All by myself." She responded proudly.

"For me?" I asked.

"Yes. All for you." She said, and added, *"Well before the food gets cold, shall we eat?"*

"Yes please." I confirmed.

I gave her a plate and we each ate. While eating, Anais became more curious about what my family was like and how I grew up. I shared what it was like at home and some stories from my past. She laughed at some. Said sorry to many, but overall, what was important to me was that she listened.

After we had both finished the pizza, we each had a slice of the mini cake. I kept the rest away.

We continued to talk about the wacky and the wonderful. After a while, she asked me if I could only open the gift from her to me tomorrow. A weird request, but everything about today had been weird anyway.

At around 5:12: pm, I said goodbye to Anais because she had to go home and get ready to meet me again at the night run. Not long after she left, my parents returned with my brother. All they had given me for my birthday was a hat that had the words 'I LUV school' on them. I was grateful, but I didn't really appreciate the lack of effort and thought they had put into my birthday.

After an awkward birthday song, I went back into my room to clean up and change into my sportswear. It was already past five, so I left the home.

Chapter
IX

"Dread is the dizziness of freedom which occurs
when ...freedom gazes down into its own possibility,
grasping at finiteness to susta."in itself."

Søren Kierkegaard

ON MY WAY TO 5th avenue, I began to get more anxious about what would take place tonight. Having Anais around all afternoon had managed to suppress the feelings I had. I was happy that those feelings didn't disrupt my day.

I quickly did a mental run of what was going down tonight. I had every detail memorised, but like Kita said there is no guarantee that everything will go smoothly. So, all we could do is hope.

When I had gotten to 5th avenue, I spotted Ms Murry sitting on the bench. She was observing a particular leaf in silence. This is the first time she has arrived early to any of the night runs.

"Hi Bertha." I said while walking up to her.

"Aha Yanis. The person I've been waiting for. How are you?" She said as she stood up from the bench.

Why would she be waiting for me?

"I'm good, and you?" I responded.

"Oh, I'm doing just fine. I have a little something for you." She turned around and picked up what looked like a book wrapped in bright red paper.

She put the parcel in my hands and pulled me towards her for a hug.

"Happy Birthday, Yanis." She whispered in my ear.

There it was. Again, she didn't smell like anything. Her voice was soft. Her words felt too fake. Despite that, she still showed interest. I hugged her back applying more force.

After a few seconds of staying in this position, we both let go. We drifted a step each backward.

"Thank you so much for this gift. I'm glad you remembered." I said.

She sat back down on the bench and I followed suit.

"It's no problem. I've had a weird feeling about today. I don't know quite what it is, but this feeling reminds me of the passing of my husband and child." She said.

"Do you think it means something bad might happen?" Please say no. I prayed silently.

She was most likely having these feelings because of our plan. Did she suspect us and wished that I say something?

From the look of things, she had no clue. So, I waited for her response;

"I don't know. I would never jump to such a horrid conclusion. No! Maybe I'm just tired. Lately, I've been having some trouble at home." She said.

Thank God she dismissed those thoughts. I was starting to fear the outcome. But now, I wondered what troubles she said she was having. Was it Corey? Or am I being too quick?

"What troubles ma'am?" I questioned.

"Nothing unusual. But I'm running low of my supply – supplies, and it's been harder trying to ration everything out so that the situation is contained until Thursday." She explained.

"Well, what happens on Thursday?" I remained inquisitive.

"It would be Klyde's birthday and I need to start preparing. I can't keep the entertainment for too long." She answered.

I had connected all the dots.

Surely Corey is the entertainment. And what does she mean she 'can't keep the entertainment'? Is she going to kill him on the day her son passed away?

If so, this means tonight is truly the last chance we have of saving him.

"Oh. I see. What will keep you entertained once the fun is all over?" I asked.

"Eh, you see, I only get this particular form of entertainment every so often. So, after it has ended, I'll be fine. Waiting is never hard." She responded faster than I anticipated.

"Yikes. I don't know about you, but I couldn't go that long without fun." I said, faking a laugh.

"Haha. Well, once you get to my age, it gets easier. So, tell me Yanis about how you've spent your birthday." She changed the subject.

So, I started telling her about my day. Before I could finish, I had to leave this conversation. Kita and Wesley called me to where they were.

"Remember your act. You have to do it early but not too early ok? We're gonna need all the time we can get." Kita reminded.

"Also make sure you send someone to come and get us so that we are aware of what has happened." Wesley added.

"So, what happens after you guys get called?" I asked.

"I have assigned people in each group to carry on if anything has to happen, so all is set." Kita answered like the real boss.

I was fine with everything, so, we left to act out our duties as group leaders. Tonight, Ms Murry will be running with Kita again. Which was good for me, so she didn't suspect anything, and so she would stay here for a while longer.

I met up with Anais after the warm-up. We greeted each other again and spoke about what we did when we separated. I mentioned once or twice that I was not feeling so well. You may think I did this to 'set' the mood, but I was genuinely feeling ill. I felt queasy like I would throw up at any given moment. Besides that, I ignored my feelings and tried to be the best group leader I could be.

When we began the run, Anais was by my side as usual. As we jogged, I started trembling. My hands were shaking and my head felt ill. I tried to hold on to my health for as long as possible. Unfortunately, it was not long before I felt like I couldn't hold it in anymore. It was still quite early into the run, but I couldn't hold it in.

I abruptly stopped running. I then attempted to go into the bushes. But before I could reach there, I threw up. Anais stopped and immediately ran up to me. As she did, so the others in my group also stopped.

"Get...Kita and... Wesley." I said in between the waste coming out of my mouth.

"Somebody, get Kita and Wesley, quick!" Anais shouted at the crowd. Quickly, one of them left.

I felt awful. I could see and smell this ghastly vomit which made me gag. Once I was sure I had finished vomiting, I pretended to fall to the ground. Anais who was standing a few meters away rushed to where I was. She sat down next to me and waited until Kita and Wesley had arrived.

When they arrived, they were shocked to see that the scene was actually real. They picked me up.

"Everybody, go back to running. There is a person to continue to lead you all." Kita instructed the crowd. She gestured to the assigned person.

"Let me come with you to make sure he is ok." Anais volunteered.

"There is no need for that. We are just taking him home. Depending on his state, we may or may not be back." Kita said being quite rude and dismissive. *"But you can always come*

and see him tomorrow." She added, upon realising Anais' shock as we walked away.

I waited until we were out of sight before dropping the act which seemed like I couldn't walk.

"*Kato was that real vomit?*" Wesley asked.

"*Everything except for my limp was real. I'm ok though. I have just had too much to eat today.*" I clarified.

I got my small bag and took out my water bottle. I rinsed my mouth and drank some water, then packed everything away - including my present from Ms Murry. Kita handed us our black outfits which we took and went behind a tree to change. Once we were finished, we made our way to the park.

As we were walking, we spoke over our plans one last time. We then spoke about what would happen after we had gotten Corey. The plan was to get a taxi and go to our home where we then consult our parents and get outside help.

Everything was carefully planned and thought over. When we reached the park, Kita guided us to the spot where she had kept all the things that we would need just hours before. She opened up the dust bin plastic, then took out the bag and opened it, revealing all of the other things. She handed us our masks and we put them on. She then handed each of us a head torch and gave Wesley the third mask for Corey and gave me the screwdriver.

We were all set. We had our gear. We had our plan.

Before Wesley and I would leave for the milk factory, we each gave Kita a hug and said our prayers.

After our prayers, I said, *"I know about your relationship with Wesley."* Directly to Kita.

"And I know about your relationship with Kita." I said directly to Wesley.

I did not give them any time to respond, for I was already walking off. Was it bad timing? Maybe, but who cares?

Wesley had no choice but to follow me. We walked in silence to the factory. Clearly, none of us had anything to say. This was the type of uncomfortable silence that I dreaded. But I just created it.

We entered the abandoned building. The smell of dust and faeces had given me the impression that something else was living here. We continued to go further in. Then, I saw it... A stray dog laying down as if it was asleep.

This was our first of many obstacles. Since Wesley was following behind me, he saw this creature after me. All we had to do was get past it without making noise. This seemed nearly impossible.

"Wesley, what the f....., what now?" I asked in a hushed voice. Anything to make sure this dog stays asleep.

"Look, let me go in first to show you how it's done."

I let him go first to demonstrate. After all, he was physically fitter than me. Wesley got up on the tips of his toes and began slowly walking past the dog. His footsteps were slow, so they did not make much of a sound. The dog was still asleep when he had made it past. Wesley had made it through. Now, all that was left was for me to do the same. Wesley stood waiting for me at the other side. He was so close, yet so far away. He gave me a reassuring smile and made hand gestures just to follow his lead.

I had done what I had observed.

Got onto the tips of my toes and walked slowly, making sure I had maintained my balance before taking my next step. When I reached the other side, I was so happy and relieved. I had done it! I had made it through. While the dog was still sleeping, Wesley and I continued to find the door.

After a while, we managed to find the door. It was two sizes down from the normal size of the door. So, to reach the handle, we both had to kneel down. It was old, so the wood had begun to rot. It looked like one touch and it would fall down. But when I tried to open the door, it seemed stuck. There was no keyhole, meaning that it couldn't have been locked. I tried again and again, but it didn't move. I gave up and let Wesley try. He also had the same problem. This door wouldn't open.

Wesley stayed on his knees thinking. He then said in a low whisper, *"Kato give me the screwdriver."*

He gave me the third mask and I gave him the screwdriver.

He moved back a little bit and positioned the screwdriver, then he put his arms in the air and struck the door knob once, then twice, then thrice and on the fourth blow, the knob fell off. He then stuck the screwdriver into the little hole the knob had fallen off from and pushed. To my amazement the door flung open. I was worried that the noise of him striking may have awoken the dog or drawn further attention, so, quickly, we crawled in, and then got up. We had to find the entrance into the basement. Once we figured out exactly where we were, it made it easier for us to locate the trap door.

Wesley used the same technique that he did with the door at the factory, except that this time, he couldn't push the door forward. He went to the edge of the door and used the screwdriver to find a crack. On finding the crack, he lifted the door up and out.

I felt useless while he was doing all of this. I wish I knew how to. I wanted to feel important. But the reality is always real ... I did not know what he was doing. I could not do what I do not know.

Once he had gotten the door open, he shined his torch down the hole,

"Kato come on. There is a ladder leading down." He announced in a tone that was accompanied by both surprise and relief.

I watched him go down the hole, legs first.

"Tell me if it's safe to come down." I said to him when he had reached the bottom.

"It's safe to come." He responded immediately.

I then followed his lead. I went down legs first as well. Once my legs had found the ladder, I made my way down. The familiar smell of nothing reminded me of where we really were, and what we were really doing. When I had gotten down from the ladder, I noticed that Wesley was looking around the room. He was at the far side of the room. I could tell because his torch light was wandering around. I myself looked around the room. There was a working station with a sewing machine and baskets of wool.

Where Wesley was, there were seven things that looked like huge cupboards covered in white clothes, all lined up next to each other.

"Wesley let's go up!" I whispered.

I had bad feelings about this place and we needed to get Corey.

"K-kato wait! You have to see this. Come quick." There was pure fear in his voice.

Nothing, but fear. His eyes were glued to one of those cupboard things.

I ran over to where he was and looked down at what he was looking at. Those were not cupboards. I felt the vomit from earlier on climb up my throat again. I couldn't vocalise what I was seeing.

There was a body of a dead teenage boy around our age laying peacefully in this glass-like casket. His limbs were sewed in a doll-like manner. I was guessing that in order to preserve the body, Ms Murry had cut them open, taken out their organs and such then stuffed the insides with some kind of material.

"Close it and let's leave." I said in a hushed voice. *"Wesley, hurry!"* I added.

He looked as if he had just snapped back to reality. He quickly covered the casket with the white cloth. He did not say a word. Since there were seven caskets, I was guessing that there were seven bodies.

This whole thing was messed up. No person should have to go through this.

The pity and sympathy I had vanished. People like Ms Murry should not exist. Yet, they do and they live normally within our society.

We soon found the stairs that led up to the first floor and climbed them. When we reached the first floor, we went through the hallways and its many rooms. After a while, we realised that we were lost. I didn't believe that after I had tried my best to memorise the layout of this place, I still ended up being lost. All we had to do was locate either the main entrance or the staircase leading up to the second floor. But instead, we kept on going around in circles.

I was getting agitated because time was running out. I had just realised that it was 7.12:12 pm. Very soon, Ms Murry would be returning home. If she did, that would mean serious trouble. Actually, that will mean our end.

After a few more minutes of arguing and getting nowhere, I found the main entrance. Wesley, who wanted to go his own way, was about to make a turn.

"Hey Wesley, come here. I think I found it." I whispered.

He turned back around and walked my way.

"Nice one Kato." He said after realising that we were not stuck in the stupid loop anymore.

I felt relevant for once. We made our way through the large empty space to the staircase leading up to the second floor.

We were so close to our goal.

We were so close to Corey.

Once we made it to the second floor, we walked straight to the room we had both heard the muffled noises coming from. Wesley handed me the screwdriver and I began picking at the lock. This task was harder than I expected, even though I did fine when we had practised it. In my head, I repeated Kita's instructions; *put it into the keyhole, then move the scre- ...*

My phone notifications went off, *"Wesley could you check the message? It might be from Kita."*

He pulled my phone out from my pocket.

At that same moment, I managed to get the door open. We heard the front door open.

Ms Murry had returned.

That was probably what Kita's message entailed.

Wesley and I quickly went into the room. There on the bed was Corey. He was either unconscious or asleep. This was my first time seeing him in months and he had changed. Other than his dark under eyes and the fact that he was wearing a different set of clothes than those he was last seen wearing, he had lost weight. The once well-built boy was now as tiny as Wesley.

Around the room, there was nothing that looked like a sign of struggle. Corey himself wasn't even restricted to the bed. The room was rather neat. Everything had a peculiar theme. Like with the rest of the house, nothing seemed to have ever been moved out of place.

While Wesley was putting the mask over Corey's face, I went to examine the closet.

In it were clothes; brand new. All bought I think, for Corey's size. This whole situation was freaking me out. I didn't like this. Not one bit.

"Kato come and help me lift him." Wesley said when he had finished masking Corey.

I rushed over to help him. While I was struggling to hold him up, I heard a noise;

Glumf,

Glumf,

Glumf,

Glumf,

Glumf,

Glumf.

They were footsteps. The sound was travelling towards the bedroom.

Wesley and I both froze, trying to hear the noise clearly one more time;

Glumf,

Glumf,

Glumf,

Glumf,

Glumf,

Glumf.

I was certain this time that it was Ms Murry.

But, how could we hear her footsteps this time? We never did.

eight?

Easy Kato, you entered the room. You are now ...

What? What are you saying eight?

Thinking fast, I looked around the room for anything I could use as a form of defense.

Time was running out. I grabbed the nearest thing around me, which happened to be a shoe horn. This shoe horn was longer than the average one. It was hard and wooden.

Glumf,

Glumf,

Glumf,

Glumf,

Glumf,

Glumf.

I quickly ran to the wall by the door and waited until the footsteps were close.

Very soon they sounded like they were right outside the door.

"Klyde honey, have you been a bad boy?" Ms Murry said when she was about to walk in.

Banshed!

She shot a bullet and missed. I didn't know she would have a gun. I didn't know.

Ms Murry hadn't noticed me yet, but she saw Wesley as he was still on the bed with Corey.

"Kato do something." Wesley said terrified not moving his gaze from the madwoman. *"Please..."*

Banshed!

She shot again. This time it hit Wesley near the collarbone. *"Ahhh fuck Kato!! Help!!"*

That's when I did it.

I moved from my current position until I was directly in front of her. She saw me and I look of confusion soon filled with hatred flashed on her face.

"Yani-"

Then, I struck her on the side of the head;

Clacks!

One blow and she dropped the gun. She attempted to grab my weapon when-

Clacks!

Another blow and she dropped to the floor. I was not sure if I had killed her, but I didn't have time to stop and think about it. I dropped the shoehorn in disgust at what I had just done.

I had to help Wesley move Corey.

Wesley was in pain and found it hard to speak. He stayed silent leaning on Corey and clutching his right shoulder.

"Kato. Wesley. Where are you?" It was the voice of Kita.

"We're up here. Up here. Come quick!" I shouted in the hopes that she would hear us.

Glumf,

Glumf,

Glumf,

Glumf,

Glumf,

Glumf.

Her footsteps were approaching the room. When she got into the room she stood at the doorway where Ms Murry lay and took in her surroundings for a second.

"Wes got hurt Kita, we have to leave now." I said to her.

"Oh my God. I'm so sorry I let this happen to you guys." She said as she rushed over to us.

She helped me carry Corey, while Wesley still had enough strength to walk.

Corey was slightly heavier than he looked, so carrying him took longer than we all predicted. Most of our struggles came when we had to walk down the stairs. His body slumped forward like he had no control.

Step-by-step, we went down.

"Put him down." Said a voice from above.

We had already finished going down all the stairs when we turned to see Ms Murry looking down at us and pointing the gun. Her hands were shaking and tears rolled down from her eyes.

I felt guilty.

"Put my son down right now or I'll shoot." The voice repeated.

We didn't respond or show fear. We just walked a little faster.

Banshed!

Banshed!

Banshed!

Banshed!

Banshed!

Banshed!

Banshed!

Banshed!

A total of eight shots were fired at us. Three missed.

Two of them hit Kita on the left arm.

Three of them hit me on my left leg.

Wesley was spared this time. So too was Corey.

We were in agony, there was blood everywhere. But we had a mission that we had to complete.

We dragged him down the stairs to the basement. Once in there, our biggest challenge would be the ladder. We could all hear Ms Murry coming, so we hid. During I bandaged my leg and Kita's arm to slow the bleeding.

Since I was the only one who could still manage to move both arms, I took a fuzz stick which was lying by her workplace and waited for her to come down the stairs.

While the others hid underneath the staircase, I was standing at the bottom.

Glumf,

Glumf,

Glumf,

Glumf,

Glumf,

Glumf.

She was coming down the stairs. Mumbling words under her breath.

Because of the lighting, I could see her but she couldn't see me. I was guessing she was all out of ammunition because she did not fire a single bullet.

When she reached the bottom of the stairs, just before she turned to switch on the lights, I spoke to her.

"Bertha, stop, please. We j-just want to help our friend." She stopped and stared blankly at me, this was not the same person.

"Yanis dear, that's not your friend. That's my son, my beloved...you won't take him from me!" She began to cry, *"You won't leave me to be all alone!"* Then she lifted her hand with the gun.

I struck her. It pained me with every blow.

Clacks!

Clacks!

Clacks!

Three times and she was out.

I limped back to where the others were hiding, *"Come let's go, we don't know how long she'll stay down."*

And we continued to move Corey.

I climbed up the ladder first then helped Wesley up. Kita stayed behind to help push Corey's body up.

"3, 2, 1, go!" I screamed as we all tried to pull/push his body forward.

We were all moaning and screaming in pain. It was a hard task, trying to push kilograms of limp flesh and muscle. Especially when gravity isn't on your side.

But like we have so far, we finally got his body through. We helped Kita up and continued down the path.

We crawled under the door, then walked through the chicken pasture. When we got into the street, I could hear police sirens. Without thinking of the police, I wondered aloud.

"You called the police?" I asked Kita.

"Yes, I did. Just before I came in to help you guys." She responded.

"All we have to do is get to the house. That's all. We can do this. We have done this." She sounded exhausted, hurt, but relieved.

We used the remaining bits of our energy and continued to walk, it felt like a walk of shame. Was it all worth it?

As we turned the corner, we saw two cop cars and three cops trying to gain access to the situation by ringing the bell of the home.

I couldn't walk any further, I sat down.

"Over here!" I shouted.

"Here!" Kita shouted after me.

All of the cops had turned to look at us, but only two approached us. They could not see our wounds in the dark, but they could see our struggle. They approached with caution, hands near their waists- near their guns.

"What are you kids doing out here so late?" The female cop asked.

"I-I'm the one who called you. We need help." Kita was stuttering. She was shaking too.

"Help? What's wrong." The female cop asked a follow-up.

"Look at us!" Wesley managed to grunt out.

"We've been shot a-a-and our friend here is unconscious. Can you please...just" She gave an indication to Corey.

"Y-you have to go in there and stop her. S-s-top Ms Murry!" I screamed. *"Please ma'am."*

They were asking too many questions. This is so dumb, do not realise that if they did not act now, she could escape and all this pain would be for nothing.

The lady signalled the man. He brought out his radio and spoke in a low hushed tone.

"Ok, you guys come with me. We have to get you to the hospital." She said, leading us to her car. *"An ambulance would take too long and we don't have time."*

Kita got into the front seat and the rest of us got into the back seat. My leg was hurting and it was only now that I noticed the bleeding had increased. The cop started the car and activated the siren then began driving. I noticed she drove with care somewhat making sure we didn't go over any rough patches.

I looked out of the window of the moving car and I felt accomplished.

Time of torture, anger, sadness and hard work had all been put into this one night. These few hours. This moment. Corey was back with us and Ms Murry will no longer pose to be a threat to other young boys. Wesley has been very quiet since his gunshot wound. But that was the least of my worries. My joy was that we were all breathing. We made it! We made it alive but all hurting.

We made it!!!

Kita looked back at me and smiled, *"We did it."* She said quietly.

I smiled back, all the problems I had with her were forgotten.

I don't know when I did, but at some point during the car ride, I fell asleep. I felt it easier to do so this time because I had no worries. No more worries.

Chapter
X

I woke up in a hospital bed.

The bright lights from above me hurt my eyes. My first reaction was to try and move, but it was quickly dismissed when I felt the sharp pain in my leg.

It was at that moment when the memories started coming back; Corey, Ms. Murry, Kita and Wesley.

Did we really do that? I dreaded the reactions from my parents. I wish I wasn't here.

I didn't like how I didn't remember entering the hospital or being changed into their horrible clothes.

"Hello?" I asked. But nobody answered, just the machines and their constant beeping.

Nobody was in my space, but I heard voices coming from my left side.

"Hellooo." I said louder.

The voices stopped when I spoke. A few seconds later, the curtain revealing the next cubicle opened and I saw my father.

He looked bad, like *"I haven't slept for days"* bad. But there he was, standing over and looking at me. He was confused but relieved at the same time.

"Kato! Are you awake?" My dad said half shouting, approaching my bed.

"No." I responded trying to be sarcastic.

Now is not the time for that.

I know, just let me be.

He sat down after patting my head and next to him was my mother. She also looked tired, but still very happy.

"My son." She gleaned while kissing my face.

Kita was on a bed like mine. She was awake and smiling. I couldn't see Isaac.

"You know that you have been sleeping for two days, straight, right?" Kita said, looking at me from her bed.

"Two whole days? New recordddd." That was amazing. I was grateful I was able to wake up.

"Amazing?? WHAT WERE YOU CHILDREN THINKING, DOING SOMETHING SO RECKLESS, AND FOR WHAT? DO YOU DO THIS SHI.. ON PUR-" My mother exploded.

I knew it was coming sooner or later.

Dad intervened, *"How about we go and get something to eat? I know you haven't eaten since getting the news. Please."* He calmed her down, she began to cry as he ushered her away.

"We will be back soon." He assured.

"Yeah, take your time." Kita responded. *"We both knew that would happened xD."*

After seconds of silence I spoke.

"So, what happened to Ms Murry?" I wonder if she was in jail or maybe she got away.

"The police actually came over yesterday to interview us. They told mother and father that Ms Murry had committed suicide by drowning herself in the fountain in the home." Kita responded with no emotion. *"You know, that fountain with the-".*

"Yes, I remember. Holy crap, I..." I tried to speak.

"Yeah, I just wish that she was alive to serve for the pain she had caused." Kita cut me off as I had done to her.

"Me too..." That and I wanted to speak to her one more time, maybe apologise for taking it all away. *"Did they find anything strange in her home?"* I asked.

"Well not that I know of. They are still investigating etc." She responded.

"Woah, must be hard." I said looking down at my hands.

"I will go into surgery tomorrow. I just thought I would give you a heads up." My sister broke it.

"Surgery for what?" I asked.

She couldn't possibly need it, I thought.

"My arm." She said lifting the bandaged arm to show me, *"They are going to cut it off rather amputate it, the bullet wounds got in too deep."*

She was sad. She was embarrassed. I would be too. I couldn't imagine not having one of my arms.

"I'm so sorry." That's all I could say.

There was nothing that could make her feel better. It was pointless.

"What's happened with Corey? A-a-and Wesley?" I asked, I was scared.

I was bothered by her silence.

"You really want to know?" She said sounding serious.

"Yes just say!" I became increasingly more worried.

"Well, after pumping his stomach, Corey's system has been rebooted and he's trying to regain his strength. As I predicted, Ms Murry used drugs to keep him under control, but it wasn't scopolamine. It was an unknown drug, something she probably made up using that sick mind of hers. The doctors still have to run testing. However, Corey is healthy and should make a fast recovery. All this is taking place in a different ward to ours, so if you had to see him, you would have to walk to the other building; which you can't." She laughed.

"I want to talk to him. Maybe someone can roll me down to where he is." This was good news.

He was alive and would be alright.

"No, you can't talk to him because he can't speak." Kita added.

"He can't speak?" I asked.

"Yes, um. Let me explain a little bit more. Although he will recover fast physically, his mental health has declined. He has

forgotten some words and how to walk. So, for the next few weeks, he will be in therapy. "She looked distanced.

"Damn..." It was a shame. I had to wait. *"And what about Wesley? Good news?"* I asked.

"Probably the best case. The bullet didn't leave any wounds, but it did hit a nerve. He is fine but has to go to therapy, not physical therapy but his overprotective parents have forced him to see a therapist and talk about the whole thing. He will most likely have back problems for the rest of his life, plus a stuttering problem."She paused.

"This isn't the ending we expected, hey?" I questioned.

"Yeah, but this is better than being dead at the hands of Ms Murry" She added.

Just like that, our relationship that seemed unfixable was fixed.

From the distance of our beds, we continued to chat about normal siblings' things. Our parents were going to be staying one more night before Kita's surgery, but after tonight they had to get some rest and be with Isaac.

I spoke to my parents about what happened that night and apologised for being quite irresponsible. My father was accepting and genuinely seemed grateful. I was ok. On her part, my mother spoke down to me about being stupid. She said I was glad to be alive. I wondered if she had spoken to Kita like this or if I had become that child again.

Before bedtime, the nurses came. They brought in our food, then checked things like our heart rate and asked us questions about if we had trouble breathing or swallowing. It was my first time in hospital and I am stuck here with my sister. I felt quite uncomfortable around them, but I was sure nothing could happen in a hospital.

"We will remove your cast tomorrow." They informed me.

Before they left for the night, I asked my parents to bring me some books and my phone the next time they came for their visit.

I woke up early in the morning to Kita tapping me on the shoulder, *"Hey, you."* She said as I was waking up.

"Hi, off to surgery soon?" I asked.

"Yeah. The nurse just left to get help. Hey, before I leave, I just wanted to tell you that I really love you and I'm scared as hell about going in." My sister really looked like she was giving up.

I had to cheer her up, *"Kita look, I love you too and I wish the best for your surgery. Maybe when you come out, we can have a normal relationship despite the Wesley and Corey drama?"*

"Kato... I'm so sorry for my actions with Wesley. You'll find it hard but I hope you forgive me." She said.

"We'll talk when you come back. Right now, the nurses are back." I said, enthusiastically pointing at them.

"Bye Kato." Kita said as the nurses pushed her bed.

"Bye Kita." I said under my breath.

I watched them disappear. I watched the room for a few minutes, gloomy without her presence. So I went back to sleep.

Later on in the morning, I woke up again and there was just an empty place. Nobody was here with me. All I could hear was the low buzzing and beeping of the machinery. I was bored. There were limited things for me to do while in the hospital.

While searching the room with my eyes, a nurse walked in with a plate of breakfast. She greeted me. I greeted back. I sat up and she put the plate on my lap,

"Do you need help?" She asked.

"No, I'm fine. Thanks." I responded briefly.

The tray had two buns, one egg, one sausage, a yoghurt and a cup of tea. She stayed for a while just adjusting things around me.

"Excuse me, ma'am? Do you have anything I can do while I wait for the doctor?" I asked.

"Well besides those magazines and the television, the only other thing I can give you is a colouring book." I said.

"Oh, you know what, could you just get me a pen and paper?" I requested.

"That I can do. I'll be right back." She stepped out.

When she left, I began eating the food. It didn't taste as bad as I expected hospital food to taste, although it was quite cold. After I had finished, I looked at a nearby desk. It had a remote for the tiny television at the corner of the room and a pile of magazines.

I picked up a magazine about health in young children and read.

A few minutes in, the nurse returned with a few sheets of paper and a single pen. She firstly removed my tray, then placed the things she had brought on my lap.

"Thank you." I said.

"No problem, do you need anything else?" She inquired.

"No this is all fine. Thank you." I expressed gratitude.

She smiled at me, then walked away.

I used the magazine that I was reading to press on as I drew. I drew how I felt the night it happened.

All the emotions. The fear. The pain. The disgust. The empathy. When I was drawing, I felt like a different person. I worked like a machine, taking just one break. I enjoyed every bit of my time.

After a few hours or minutes, I am not sure because I had lost track of time. While completing my last sheet, the doctor arrived.

"Good afternoon, Kato." The doctor said.

Afternoon already?

"Good afternoon, doctor." I responded, putting down what I was doing. *"What's your name?"* I asked.

"Doctor Fidel. As you were told, I will be taking off your cast today. Last time we checked; you had a few broken bones. With help, I'm sure you'll be able to walk again." The doctor assured me.

"Oh, that's good to hear Doc." I responded.

"Nurse please." He called.

A nurse different to the one who served me breakfast entered the room with a wheelchair. She helped me out of bed and placed me into the wheelchair. She wheeled me out.

The hospital was big, with many doors, rooms and many nurses.

As I was being pushed around, I thought of Kita. I hoped she was ok. It must be scary for her to go into surgery all alone. But I knew that she was strong and capable of getting through this small challenge.

A few minutes later, we arrived at a room. The nurse helped me and put me on the table. She then stood and watched at a distance. I lay down on my back and waited.

The doctor approached my cast and started fiddling around with the cast, before leaving and coming back with something that looked like a pizza cutter. He turned the machine on at a click sound. The blade started spinning around. He then started cutting the cast little by little. He seemed very cautious.

After he had finished the inside of my leg, he moved to the outside. He performed the same task, and when he had finished, he took a pair of scissors and began to cut along the line. It was a long process, but I was anxious to see and actually, feel how my leg had healed.

When he was finished, I was disappointed that I was not allowed to see my leg just yet. I lay on my back while he felt my leg.

"Can you feel this?" He asked while squeezing my low leg.

"Yes." I responded.

"How about this?" He asked.

"Yes." I said.

"Wiggle your toes please." He instructed.

I wiggled them.

"Great. You have gained some strength back. We're all lucky the bullet hadn't hit your fibula or you would be left unable to walk for the rest of your life." He said.

"Thanks?" I said, confused.

"So, what happens next is to start with some light exercises. We will gradually move on to heavier things. In maybe a month or two, you will be able to run again." He explained.

"Oh, that's great!" I was happy, and I asked, *"When will we start?"*

"Next week. Until then, you won't have a cast on and any major movement done on your leg could lead to a more serious injury. So, you'll have to stay in bed. Nurse." He said.

The nurse came and put me back into the wheelchair.

"Thank you so much Doc." I said.

"It's my duty Kato. Get some rest." He responded.

When I arrived in my room, I saw my mother, my father, Isaac and ... Anais.

I hadn't seen Anais since the scene during the night run. I had no time to think of what to say or to make sure I looked presentable because I had received no warning. Actually, even with a warning, how do I prepare on a wheelchair?

Anais was sitting down watching me. This made me feel uncomfortable. I had no idea what she would think of me or this situation. Would she feel betrayed? Lied to? Or angry?

After the nurse had lifted me onto the bed, we shared our greetings and I talked about my day. They all listened and contributed with their own thoughts. So far, everything was going smoothly. My mother handed me my bag.

"Anais insisted she came around and helped me choose your favourites. She's been helping us look after Isaac when we have things to do." My mother explained.

I looked at Anais and she was staring at me ... with the same gaze the day of my birthday. This time, the expression her eyes showed were different. They seemed hungry for knowledge.

"Yeah Kato, Anais is like the best person ever. We do so many things together." Isaac said, boasting.

We continued to talk about the little things in all of our lives. It was peaceful. No shouting, no frustration or anything like that. I didn't feel out of place. I didn't feel that I was less or more.

"Mother, father. Can I speak with Anais privately?" I asked.

My father understood and left. My mother hesitantly followed, dragging Isaac with her.

Anais got up from her seat and leaned on the side of my bed.

"I missed you." She told me.

"I missed you too." I responded.

"How are you?" She asked.

"Better than I had expected. Everything is running smoothly. The doctor said that I am making a speedy recovery and I should be able to walk really soon." I told her.

"You don't know how happy I was to see you alive. I was so worried. I came to the hospital the morning after it happened, but you were still asleep." She explained.

"Nobody ever told me you came..." I protested.

"Oh well, that doesn't matter anymore. -" She said.

We talked about the event and how I had felt. She expressed her thoughts on the whole thing. She didn't have any feelings of anger. She was as happy as she would have been on any other day. We spoke about Ms Murry and who she was as a person. We both felt that it was unfair that she just got away with what she had done and had to face no consequences. Anais explained that she was certain that Ms Murry was the only person she hated in the entire world.

I gave her the photos I drew earlier on and explained to her what they each meant.

I then opened up the bag my mother had given me earlier. In it was my favourite book and a few other things; my sketchbook with pencils, my phone, a few sweets and my diary.

It would be all I needed to survive the next few weeks.

In the bag was also the present Ms Murry gave me. I saw fit that I had to open it now.

"What's that?" Anais asked me.

"I-It's the gift Ms Murry gave me for my birthday." I said.

"You want to open it?" She looked surprised and confused.

"Yeah." I said lightly.

I tore the wrapping paper to reveal a bright red cover with words on the picture written in gold. I opened it and on all the pages were pictures. Random pictures I thought they were. At the bottom of each picture was a little column with words in a foreign language written on them. It sure would be a hassle to translate all of them, but I am looking forward to doing so with Kita.

"What is it?" Anais asked.

"A picture book." I responded.

"Oh." She said, sounding puzzled.

"Thanks for looking after Isaac." I diverted.

Anais didn't respond. She just stared at me, and then out of nowhere, she kissed me. I didn't kiss her back nor did I pull away. It wasn't a long kiss, but enough had been displayed. When she pulled away, she looked at me smiling.

"That was-"

I was interrupted by a doctor walking in, *"Excuse me, I am looking for the parents of Kita Sterik. Do you know where they are?"*

My parents had left for the food court.

"Yes. I do. They went into the food court." Anais answered.

"Thank you." The doctor said and left in a rush.

"What do you think he wants?" I asked Anais.

"Probably to sign some stuff regarding Kita's surgery. She should be coming back to your ward soon." She responded.

All my worries had been dismissed and we continued to talk. I showed her some of my drawings and read her some of my poems.

For some reason, eight and I have not had an encounter for a day.

Anyway, I was reading her one poem, when we were interrupted ... again.

My parents and Isaac walked into the room. Isaac was in my father's arms while my mother leaned against his chest.

My mother was ugly. She was crying. She was shouting out thin phrases and hitting my father in anger. Isaac was crying. I knew what had happened without having to be told. I looked over at Anais as she watched them approach my bed in terror. She took my hand and started squeezing it.

I looked at the big clock on the wall.

It was 6:20 pm.

"Kato, Kita is dead." Said father.

I told you.

Anais put her head on my chest, waiting for a reaction but I felt nothing.

The End

The
Puzzle

Stacey will love to see what words you get from this puzzle. Please share a picture of your finding @staceyfru on social media.

```
R W V M P T G D C O R E Y U P I Y S
C E Z I V U R P S O A T U B U W G Q
B O A D M H E H C M G N D S O D B T
T D C D D H W I E V E D A X Q O Q N
J I P L I W U L H H F L B I K H K N
R I H E K N Y O H V O S L J S I C S
G M X B A E G S G D U T U Y M P T G
Y L O U T U N O F G N A M G C C U A
K S K R O F W P F M D C E X Q A E H
N R G G C R F H K D Y E R M T O T I
Q K S J D U W Y F E N Y U Q J N M S
V G P W E S L E Y A M I S S I N G O
```

ANAIS	KATO	KITA
FRU	PHILOSOPHY	READING
MISSING	WESLEY	FOUND
STACEY	COREY	MIDDLEBURG
BOOKS	SMELLY CATS	

Testimonial

Born to express herself and her innate wisdom in writing and public speaking, by age 13, Stacey Fru was the first International Multiple Award-Winning Child Author who wrote her first book Smelly Cats at the age of 7. The book is approved as suitable learning material by the Department of Basic Education. At age 12, Stacey was honoured by the Egyptian President Abdel Fattah el-Sisi as Africa's Youngest Most Promising Youth. She was also named Global Child Prodigy in India. At 13, she was shortlisted for the International Peace Prize for Children. Stacey is the youngest author whose book, Tim's Answer was translated into Braille and DAISY formats by Blind SA in 2019. She was the youngest founding member of the Wits University Center for Multilingual Education and Literacy at age 9. Stacey is a talented public speaker, guitarist, brand ambassador, mentor, analyst and philanthropist. This activist in literacy, anti-abduction, anti-kidnapping, anti-trafficking and anti-abuse is well-travelled and internationally acclaimed with over 30 International, Presidential, Ministerial, Premier, Legislative or Parliamentary, Mayoral,

Academic, Non-governmental, Media, Brand, Heroine, Individual and Business awards and recognitions. To avoid shining alone, Stacey celebrates the achievements of other children across Africa during the Annual AfrICAN Children of The Year Awards hosted by her own foundation - the Stacey Fru Foundation.

These testimonials from around the world, in form of comments, praises, poems and stories, gives you the opportunity to see Stacey through the eyes of children and adults, whose lives she has impacted so profoundly. It is a fitting tribute.

Other Books

by

Stacey Fru

SMELLY CATS

Smelly Cats was written without her parents' knowledge. It is about 2 cats who are cousins. It portrays the common challenges of different socio-religious and academic backgrounds and challenges posed by geographical locations to the two on a daily basis. Stacey's book also depicts that even though the cats come from the same family, they are bound to have differences due to who they are. The constant fights are real reflections of daily lives. Want to know more?

BOB AND THE SNAKE

This book is about Bob, a boy who loves snakes with his whole heart. His birthday is coming up and he is super happy because he heard his parents talking that they may buy him a real snake for his birthday. Bob learns to respect his parents by disrespecting them. To her; "no matter how much they try, children will always be

naughty and parents will always be hard." Hungry for more? Order copies.

SMELLY CATS ON VACATION

This book is a follow-up of 'Smelly Cats.' Smelly Cats on Vacation is about Mack and his father's fantastic holiday in Namibia. Mack and Mark remained mischievous throughout the holiday. Unfortunately, Mack comes back to South Africa with an injury. What happened to the girls in the book Smelly Cats? When schools reopen, smelly cats go to High School.

WHERE IS TAMMY?

Many other children including 6-year-old Tammy depends on grown-ups, to become grown-ups themselves. Unfortunately, like many children, Tammy was taken away by strangers as he walked beside his father. Tammy's reunion with his overjoyed father hours later, gives Stacey an

opportunity to teach children about Safety and Security different situations and to remind grown-ups that child kidnapping is real. Play-Your-Part! Make the world a better place.

TIM'S ANSWER

Why do many of us look out of our communities for role models? Stacey upholds the African IdenStity. She invites readers to look within Africa for role models. In this book, Tim fails to find a role model during a school project. He goes overseas to search in American and Europe, but no luck. Finally, the disappointed Tim comes back to South Africa only to find out that Tata Nelson Mandela is his number one role model. Play-Your-Part! Be a better role model.

THEMES IN STACEY'S BOOKS

Illiteracy

Poverty/Inequality

Religion

Jealousy

Ignorance

Safety and Security

Respect

Kindness

Honesty

Selflessness

Love

Health

Family and Friendship

Difference

Abuse

Role Models

Human Trafficking

Kidnapping

Culture

About the Author

Stacey Fru is a 15-year-old International Multiple Award-Winning Child Author named a Global Child Prodigy. In 2019, she was honoured by the Egyptian President as one of 5 Most Promising African Youths. Stacey wrote her 1st book "Smelly Cats" at age 7 and has since dedicated a portion of her life to reaching out, inspiring and educating people.

Stacey founded the Stacey Fru Foundation in 2018 and has been impacting the lives of underprivileged children in her community.

In 2022, Stacey was elected as the Junior MMC of Community Development within the Johannesburg Student Council. She is a passionate learner at Sacred Heart College, anxiously waiting to become an adult.

During the COVID-19 Pandemic that took the world by surprise back in 2020. South Africa was placed on lockdown. Stacey wrote this book during the first few weeks of lockdown. This is the first book that she wrote outside her bedroom. Their father redesigned their study room during this period, so that he, his wife and all their children could sit together. For this reason, he took out computers from the children's bedrooms. Every single work and school day, the entire family sat together in this room. The mother and father work and the children attend online classes. When classes were over, the children went out for snacks, which they often ate together while conversing. They would chill, relax and read books. Often after reading, the other children would sneak into their devices, while Stacey would sneak into her newly created writing corner; their dining room.

You can visit Stacey online at www.staceyfrufoundation.org.za or on social media (@staceyfru).